Came

City of Death

Books by Cameron Strike

Becker & Zonk

#1 - Decapitator

#2 - Gone Boys

3 - House of Carnage

Berlin Noir

#1 - City of Death

#2 - Devil's Mountain

Contents

And I guess that's all OK if you're one of those tormented-soul detectives with a drink problem and a broken marriage, who's had some big trauma in his childhood and is searching after his feminine side, or whatever that load of old toot goes.

Robert Rankin, *Waiting for Godalming*

Prologue

The guy sat opposite me, sweating like a pig. It wasn't particularly warm in the bar and he'd been sitting there for some time. He was just nervous. And hopping mad. At me.

Which was reasonable.

I was about to wrangle a whole lot of money out of him and he didn't like it because he loved his money. Much more than he loved his wife. That didn't mean much because he didn't love his wife at all. Which was why he now had to fork out.

We were in *Billy Wilder's*, the trendy tourist trap in the Sony Center, Potsdamer Platz, filled with black and white photographs from the Grand Old Man who had been a reporter for the *B.Z.* when he was young. There wasn't much happening; it was daytime and off-peak. It was drizzling outside. I was drinking scotch neat. My guest had ordered a large beer which dripped moisture just as he did.

The photos spread out in front of him were not black and white. They were high-quality images, snapped by yours truly two days earlier. Each showed my guest and one other person in the nude. Aesthetically speaking, they made very different impressions. The young lady was a whole lot more photogenic.

"How the hell did you do that?" he spluttered. He didn't whine but I had a feeling that he might throw up. As a precaution, I changed my position so I could leap out of the way quickly. I had a new shirt on and it cost a bomb.

"The camera was permanently installed in the hotel

room," I explained patiently. "Why did you always book the same room?"

He didn't reply. I could see he was chewing it over. Exploring his options. But he finally had to ask the crucial question.

"What do you want?"

I smiled at him kindly. Well, I don't really have a kind smile; I have a shark's mouth that doesn't turn upward. It was probably more of a sympathetic grin. It has no effect whatsoever on women, but it works on guys like him.

"You and your secretary are a very creative couple," I began, "so you can probably figure out what I want to ensure these images don't get into the hands of your wife. By the way, she asked me to get evidence of your unfaithfulness. I can either give the pictures to her - there are also digital copies of them - or to you."

His face twisted into a mass of skin lumps.

"How do I know that you won't cross me? I mean, that there are no negatives, everything is digital?"

He was right. Yet again modern technology was complicating things unnecessarily. I would probably have to get a Smartphone. I thought it completely pointless to use the Internet while out and about but there was no alternative, in my line of work it was occasionally quite useful. Though not quite as useful as the gun in my jacket. Maybe Apple will design a gun-app soon. Sure thing.

"I can't offer you any security," I replied. "If you're not comfortable with the situation, you could always end it by coming clean to your wife."

His jaw tensed as he gritted his teeth. That was obviously not an option.

"Or... you pay the parking ticket."

That's what I call my incidental income. I always adapt it to fit the economic situation of the delinquent. In this case, it was 20,000 Euros. I could have asked for more, the man was a millionaire, the Berlin version of a tycoon, as they were called in Donald Duck comics and FDP party programs. With "Berlin version" I mean it was not comparable to companies in Baden-Württemberg, more like a company that made beer pumps that were exported globally. He was a good guy, I had nothing against him. What he did with his secretary or, more accurately, she with him, was his business and he was discreet. I found the black rubber instrument shaped like a giant black hand really funny. She had worked his butt beautifully with it. It looked like real hard work and I hoped the lady got a decent bonus for it.

"How about ten grand? I could confess to my old lady, then you wouldn't get a penny and I could charge you for extortion."

Now that really deserved respect! He was trying to haggle! I'm not much of a patriot, but this attitude has made Germany great again, hasn't it? Other countries base their economy on debt and senseless consumption; Germans check the digits after the decimal. I now liked the chubby little perv a bit more. Too bad that it cost him five more grand.

"I'm afraid that's now twenty-five thousand. Stop quibbling. You won't tell your wife or the police. Remember, divorce is expensive; your party will throw you out and in the end it'll be your word against hers."

He fumbled through the photos.

"Not if I show these to the police..." he muttered thoughtfully and menacingly at the same time.

"It won't come to that," I replied nonchalantly. "I'm afraid you have to decide right away. I have an appointment with your wife in half an hour, she's probably already on the way to my office."

I wasn't bluffing. I was quite happy just to pocket my fee. Right now I was in good economic shape.

"How am I supposed... Would you like a check?" There was a glimmer of hope in his eyes. Smart aleck.

"Come on, wise guy," I laughed and downed my Scotch. That reminded him of his beer, and he emptied half the glass. He avoided my eyes, as he had during the entire conversation. I always tried to make eye contact but not everyone has the nerve to respond, especially not guys who feel guilty and at the same time want to punch me in the face. I wasn't afraid of that. I'm not a top athlete, but I can hit hard if necessary. German entrepreneurs also never make a scene in public. That would be a sign of weakness.

I explained, "The bottom line is, I know you have several accounts which you can access online. You could pay immediately, either with your mobile or from a computer next door."

There was a *Dunkin Donuts* next door and they had an internet cafe on the first floor. I had chosen our meeting place very wisely.

There was no escape. All in all twenty-five grand was a very reasonable price to pay so he could continue his dolce vita. And maybe he had learned his lesson. Marital vows are important.

What next? That lousy blackmailer had the nerve to moralize; who does he think he is? Take it easy. I'm no saint, we all have our failings. It's not as if I do this type of thing regularly. I'm a real detective. I have mastered my craft and help my clients. But I feel that now and then you must think of yourself. I would, at some point, like to own a small motor boat and sail down the River Havel. You wouldn't begrudge me that, would you?

The transfer to my special account took just a minute. I picked up the photos and promised the man that he would never hear from me again. He didn't object to my taking the pictures, he seemed to regard it as a cleaning up operation. The nightmare was over, that chapter was closed.

"Have a good one," I said cheerfully, leaving behind a man who still couldn't quite believe what had hit him. He was finishing his beer as I grinned at him through the window.

Twenty minutes later his wife was sitting in my office. I carefully laid out the photos on my desk and, with deeply felt regret, revealed the terrible truth.

"I'm sorry, but you were quite right. Your husband is cheating on you."

Bad dog

I won't bother you with my life story. I'm not into regression therapy. But I will tell you a few things about me now and again if I feel it necessary. You may have noticed that I am not your Mr. Average. I never was. This may sound arrogant, but I'm not claiming to be a better person. I just have a different approach to life.

I was aware of this quite early. When I was twelve, a TV movie was filmed nearby. A whodunit, *Tatort*. Can't remember which episode. They're always the same, like prison food. Germans are lifelong prisoners of their TV industry, the only escape is to learn English or to hope that a good American or English series is synchronized accurately and then broadcast. I remember almost all the episodes of *Moonlighting*, but not a single *Tatort*.

One of the props for an outdoor shot was a mailbox. It wasn't real, but it looked real, and the film crew forgot to take it with them when they left. I noticed this the next day, and was wondering what to do when I saw someone post a letter in the box and a few minutes later yet another. Within the hour about twenty letters, including some bulky large-format ones, had been dropped in the fake mailbox.

You may say: Eckstein, you tit, why didn't you tell them so they didn't lose their mail? Legitimate question. I suppose most people would react that way, but I considered other options. What was in the envelopes anyway? Greeting cards? Vows of love? Chain letters?

Money even?

These thoughts raced through my brain. Shame on me. Even more shameful: I went home and picked up my dad's small leather tool bag, the one he called his "Detlev-purse". I had no idea that Detlev was a synonym for our penis-appreciating friends - I thought it was the regular term for a black bag with a hand strap and a small selection of tools; it included a spanner that matched perfectly the screw holding the mailbox to the wall. The crew had improvised; a real mailbox would presumably be more securely fitted. Fortunately.

Talking about mailboxes - are they still around? Before the internet era people transmitted information on sheets of paper which was delivered, for a small consideration, to the recipients by a transport service. These letters were collected in large yellow boxes and... Got it? Alright, then.

As soon as it was it dark, I moved. I unscrewed the box, put the loot in a safe place, our basement. I was too young to know how to pick a lock (now my record is five a minute), but I figured that the box had to be upside down to get at the spoils.

Most of it was mundane stuff, but there was a juicy erotic letter from a young woman to a young man. Even at twelve I found the subject intensely interesting, but stopped reading when the women declared she longed for the "taste on her tongue" of her lover's "manliness". I found that absolutely disgusting (now my record is five times a night), definitely not for me. The 10 D-Mark note a grandmother sent to her grandson for his First Communion was different. I found that really tightfisted, (I had bagged a total of 300 D-Mark for mine and had no idea what Communion was all about), I was really shocked!

I kept the tenner.

Now don't look at me like that. I was twelve, I was a

child and children are born evil. When I hear people refer to the "innocence" of children, I wonder if they've ever met a child. Not having sex doesn't make you an innocent angel - a recluse with strong wrists more likely. Or to give it the official term: "monk".

I bought my first magazine for sexual health with the money; it was called *St. Pauli Nachrichten*. There was very little about events in that notorious part of Hamburg. I found the mag very enlightening; it has, in fact, shaped my taste in women. As a consequence, I started quite late with sex - young girls don't have breasts which can double as swimming floats. My taste in women is more sophisticated now, but I was just twelve then!

The experience didn't lead to a criminal career. I've never been in jail, at least not for more than one night. Taking hard-earned Catholic bribes off another boy about my age, implicated me. He probably got his money in the end and a bit more on the side as compensation.

But I can't deny that this episode was one of the key moments in my life. I've never spoken to anyone about it. Neither my parents nor any of my friends, I had a feeling they might disapprove. Adult professionals with uniforms and / or serious faces might then have intervened. I could live without that.

I did the mail box trick a few times, until it was finally picked up by the film crew. I don't know if my actions significantly affected anyone's life but, to my vindication, I re-sent a couple of letters that seemed important. I really did. Believe me.

My life carried on as before. And why not? Have you never stolen anything from a shop? Or pinched money from your parents' desk? It doesn't necessarily make you a mass murderer. But I had learned something about myself: I was pretty devious. A risk-taker. A combination of characteristics that have served me well time and again. And have landed me in hot water just as often.

I wasn't good at school, I was disinterested. I knew I would never use most of the stuff once I had my A-levels. Absolutely true. I am grateful for my English classes because today I read and speak that silly, primitive language fluently, but I don't owe it all to my school because my final grade was a Four. The weakest of my courses, I was better in philosophy, computer science and art, even though my art teacher was a so-called “wanker”. A narcissistic hypocrite who detested anyone who didn't consider spots of color on canvas or fatty lumps on chairs art. My good English is down to the DVD. British sitcoms like *Black Adder* and *Red Dwarf* taught me that there is something better than lousy German comics who wouldn't be allowed to do even a warm-up at a BBC show.

My parents wanted me to study, of course, but whatever for? Nothing interested me. I had been forced through thirteen years of school, why should I hang out in classrooms again? Did it never end?

Purely by chance I landed in the security industry. I was a natural athlete and could hold my own in a physical confrontation. I settled in very quickly and, because I was over-qualified, very soon had a senior position.

And was given a gun license.

In case you query that, it is not common practice. In Germany very few security guards in the private sector have firearms. What for? Very few German law breakers have firearms. This is not Yemen, Chad or the United States of America. Some criminals do use firearms, but on whole shoot-outs are extremely rare. Now and again a policeman bites the dust; being armed is of no use to him at all.

I own a Walther P22, the successor to the classic James Bond weapon Walther PPK, a neat, small caliber handgun for protection. I have permission to "hold" a weapon, as they say, and it wasn't easy getting it. I was able to demonstrate that I was in more danger than Joe Public - a prerequisite, coupled with a stable personality and a steady hand.

As a former security provider I was easily able to prove to officials that I had to deal with quite a few shady characters. Furthermore, I had been attacked on my way home one night. It was a guy I had caught pinching stuff in a hotel lobby. I managed to overpower him, he was given three months in the clink and I was allowed to keep my gun license, even though I was now a freelance private investigator. I had, of course, paid the guy handsomely and in advance for his services. It was worth it.

That's why I don't worry if my "parking ticket"-payers know who I am. I can assess just how dangerous people get. One short comment on unfaithful husbands: they are wimps. The tough guys you need to be wary of don't invent cock-and-bull stories so their wives don't suspect anything. They either don't start a relationship or, more usually, are faithful, or they don't care if she does find out.

This time, though, things got a bit out of hand. A little later a few of my photos landed in a newspaper. I say "newspaper", it was actually the *Kurier*. The fall guy was not only a little tycoon, but also a local conservative handshaker. I had nothing whatsoever to do with it. His wife, though, had stormed out of my office in a towering rage.

My office is in Charlieburg. That's what I call Charlottenburg, even if no one else does, I find it amusing. It's located in a rear building. At the time I was offered an office facing the street with a large bay window which would have matched my desk perfectly. But the word “sniper” kept flashing through my brain so I moved into the rear building.

I won't name the exact location; I hate doorbell pranks and crazy adulterers with bull terriers on a leash.

Like this one here, for instance.

“You bastard! You goddamned motherfucker!”

It was late, the sun had set and the lighting in my bolt hole wasn't good. But I got the picture immediately: hubby stood in the open door, dressed in Adidas' finest, panting heavily from the effort of barging up three flights of stairs. I wasn't afraid of him, not a bit.

The exact opposite was true of the bull terrier.

You know, these critters that look like four-legged hitmen? Not huge, but sturdy, with nasty little eyes and teeth like a reef shark? His was a particularly nasty specimen: mainly white with a few black spots and obviously very belligerent.

“How dare you?” his master bellowed. “I'm ruined, you asshole!”

I wanted to reply that he had only himself to blame, that it had nothing to do with his ticket, that eventually his wife had done what she had always deemed appropriate. But the vibrations I sensed led me to believe that my guest was not in a mood to discuss values.

“Listen,” I began and slowly got up from my chair, “I

understand your predicament, but...”

“Shut up!”

He bent down and let Snoopy off his leash. The critter seemed to know what was coming, anticipation was written all over his cold, soulless mug.

“Frightened?” He grinned and swung the leash around. “May I introduce you? Philip Eckstein, this is Fausto. Fausto, that's your dinner.”

“Hello, Fausto,” I snarled, glancing toward the coat rack on the wall, just one step away from my guest. That's where my coat was and my gun was in my coat. Beyond reach.

When I come in I should, of course, put the gun in the desk so that it is within reach, but sometimes I forget and I don't want to become too paranoid.

Fatso had savored his triumph and was now ready for action. He bent his knees slightly, then pointed at me with his outstretched arm.

“Fausto – get him!”

With a joyous yelp Fausto jumped on the desk. He didn't bark, he hissed like a puma. The difference in height seemed to confuse him; he probably usually worked from the calves up to the testicles. That one second was enough for me.

I ducked down (like a classic action hero) and slipped under the desk, which was wide enough to crawl into. Fausto barked, angry at this missed opportunity. I heard him jump off the table but I couldn't see where. What I could see were Fatso's adidas Treads (I really respect brand loyalty), as they raced towards my face.

“Hang on, pal!” the dog lover yelled. He kicked violently but as he was not a sporty type his sole just touched my head and didn't hurt much. I rolled towards my coat.

"Get him! Fausto! Get him!"

The guy was hyperventilating, his blood lust was stronger than that of his best friend. I tried to get up when I suddenly felt an excruciating pain. I lay on my stomach, I couldn't see what was going on, but it wasn't necessary. You can't avoid noticing it when two dozen sharp teeth slam into your lower leg.

I yelled briefly and clenched my teeth. One thing I knew about fighting dogs: the more you kick the more they bite. I endured the pain for a few seconds, I heard the dog growl and its owner snigger.

"You poor thing," he sneered "it doesn't hurt, does it?"

"Not a bit," I replied, "I had an itch there anyway."

Just a meter in front of me was the foot of the coat stand. The loaded gun was out of sight and I didn't want to look too obviously in its direction. The beast was the main problem; it was slowly working towards my sweet little butt, its anticipated main course.

I changed strategy and said: "You won't get away with this, you'll land in jail, wanna bet?"

"Wanna bet that I don't give a damn?" the guy replied. "I have excellent lawyers. You shouldn't have attacked me. It's your word against mine. Who's your lawyer, motherfucker?"

Fausto had calmed down a bit now his owner's tone was quieter. He was enjoying his revenge and was in no hurry. The beast now bit my thigh, with more relish than any lady with similar thoughts. I was glad I was lying on my stomach otherwise this chapter of my life might have reached a sorry end. New strategy.

"You feel really tough even though it's the beast that does the real work, huh?"

He didn't respond immediately. For a moment you could only hear the dog snarling and growling, he enjoyed his job, but didn't know what to do next. His master did though.

The first kick caught my ribs, then the fat bastard put his foot in my back.

"I'm a match for you anytime, you half-pint!"

"Really," I replied in choked tone. "Only when I'm messed up, as I am now?"

"Fausto, stop."

His tone was remarkably calm and Fausto obeyed instantly. The pain was severe and I couldn't sense whether blood seeping out or not. My trousers were of durable, black corduroy (always the cool cosmopolitan playboy) and had probably prevented the worst. That was good because my antique Persian carpet hadn't been cheap.

I felt reasonably capable but didn't want to show it. I turned over slowly and leaned on my forearms. Fausto sat two feet away from me next to the desk with his tongue hanging out. His boss looked at me, distrustful but confident of victory. That was the idea: The dog would incapacitate me so he could give me the once over. That explained the jogging suit.

"Okay," he grinned, "Get up. I can't wait."

I avoided his eyes as I straightened up. I winced in pain as I put my full body weight on my leg - after all corduroy isn't a suit of armor. I cried out in pain, exaggerating slightly, and pretended I needed support.

"Don't fall over, you bum, although I'll finish you off

on the floor, if necessary!"

It wasn't necessary. I staggered sideways shielding the coat on the rack with my body. A precise grab at the specially tailored inside pocket and my little darling was in my hand. The gun, I mean.

I didn't think twice, it was quite clear what had to be done. In the movies, the hero behaves decently and gives his tormentors the opportunity to retire peacefully. But this was a fight. A real fight. And if you want to win a fight, the opponent must be disarmed first and foremost.

It took just one second. I swung around and fired.

"Noooo..!" Fatso shrieked.

"Iiiiuuuuu..." yowled Fausto, very briefly.

The dog was killed instantly. Even I was impressed, the bullet hit his white monster head, slightly to the left, next to his huge, curved nose. They say animals are never to blame, the owners are responsible, dogs are blameless. Rubbish. Intelligent animals have character, they are not automatons. Fausto was a bastard and now he was dead. I hoped his blood wouldn't drip onto the carpet. I wasn't bleeding either, a result of my good manners.

"Don't move," I growled at Fatso who was lurching between shock and anger trying to grasp when the tide had suddenly turned. I stood safely on my feet but the pain would keep me occupied for a few days. Luckily I had been given a tetanus injection. Have you had one? Check your vaccination certificate; it saves thousands of lives each year.

I didn't point the gun at the guy. They go off damn easy when you're nervous and my adrenaline was in party mode.

“Please, don't hurt me,” he gasped and I wanted to shoot him for using that stupid cliché.

“You forced your way in,” I said quietly. “Unlawfully and with intent to injure me. Now I can do what I want. I know exactly how to twist things so it looks as if you attacked me. That's a no-brainer.”

We eyed each other and both knew that I was serious. I had never killed a man and had no ambitions in that direction. There was a lot at stake. The police would have a few questions, for instance why he was here at all, what was the connection. And then there was the bank transfer to my Special Account. I was risking my neck.

“Listen,” I said and pointed the gun at his feet. “You fuck off now. I'll look after the doggie. With luck and your amazing lawyers you'll survive this crap. But for now, not only do you know where I live, I know where you live. And where you work, where you screw your secretary - or enjoy being thrashed by her - and I know where you go for a munch. And only one of us possesses a gun. Is that clear enough?”

He nodded. Pale, trembling and dripping with sweat he stumbled toward the door. He didn't even glance in the direction of his beloved dog. He charged to the stairwell and I heard him pounding down the stairs.

My neighbors had heard nothing apparently, but that wasn't surprising. The offices were already empty, the apartments further above, so I was almost alone in the house.

I put the gun in a desk drawer; I would clean it properly later. Fausto lay on the floor like a sack of potatoes. There was very little blood from the gunshot wound. I grabbed some tissues and wrapped them round his head to protect my carpet. A quick inspection showed that my blood hadn't seeped onto it either. Only then did I lower myself onto the leather couch and carefully take off my trousers.

I was bleeding, the teeth had sunk in quite deep, there were holes in my trousers, but the damage was minimal. I limped into the bathroom. I had the essentials for wound dressing in the medicine cabinet: antiseptic, iodine, bandages. I treated the nastiest cuts, then went back to the couch and wrapped myself generously in bandages.

I was just about to get up and pour myself a drink when I realized I was no longer alone.

I hadn't locked the door and in the glare of the hallway light stood a figure.

“You made a mistake, Herr Eckstein.”

Amanda

She was in her late 20s, early 30s or even older. To be honest, this is my handicap: guessing a person's age. These days people do absurd things to their faces. Some inject nerve poison, officially considered a biological weapon, under the skin: Botox. A single gram of it is said to be enough to depopulate a city.

I'm 38, but I don't look it. Mostly because I seldom smile and avoid the sun. This blonde's face had such a translucent radiance that I actually needed a few nanoseconds before checking the rest of her body. An extremely pleasant process. Even though she was wearing a pretty blue Caban, I could identify substantial curves - I'm not only a detective, but also a shallow libertine. Below the jacket generous hip and thigh curves were sheathed in very tight jeans and continued downward ending in two high-heeled shoes which I considered inappropriate for the wet weather.

“Are you done, or shall I turn around?”

She was smiling, but the expression in her eyes revealed a different temperament. It was a challenging gaze and I always take on any challenge.

“Thanks, but I'd prefer it if you went down on all fours.”

After all it was my office, I don't let a sex bomb (are they still called that?) who waltzes in unexpectedly put me on the defensive. She'd need to bring a bull terrier to do that.

She laughed and came into the office. The body of the beast was in her blind spot, I would save that little surprise for later. I was sitting, trouserless, on the couch and out of politeness started to get up, but with a "Sh-sh" and a slight wave of the hand, she indicated I should stay where I was. You know the drill: if a woman capable of modeling underwear for the Otto Catalogue waves her hand, you obey. No idea how they manage it, but they know it works and use it constantly.

They don't often do what you would like them to do, that is fall on their knees in front of a trouserless stranger.

But she did.

The last meter she actually completed on all fours with her gaze directed at my crotch.

I can't remember exactly what I was thinking at that moment. Something between "Help, a lunatic" and "Wow, so there is an easier way." But, unsurprisingly, it wasn't like that.

"The bandage is too loose," she muttered and started to re-bind it. "It'll just slip down."

"Oh, thank you," I said.

"Keep still."

I kept still. I met her just a minute ago and she had conquered me already. Who says it's a men's world?

It took her a couple of minutes, but even if the process wasn't pain-free, the result appeared to be very professional.

"You've done this before?" I asked as she stood up.

"I'm a very experienced woman."

"You don't look like one."

An idiotic lie. She looked as though she might do a parachute jump over the Serengeti at three in the morning while reading *Cosmopolitan*. She ignored the reply.

"Where are your trousers?"

"Why, do I need them?"

She laughed softly and crossed her arms.

"I'm afraid so. Unless you prefer not to talk to me."

"Nothing better than that," I assured her solemnly. "My trousers... are over there."

I noticed, while speaking, that my trousers were almost next to the animal corpse. My guest looked over and discovered them both.

"Is that your dog? What's his name... oh!"

She had noticed it almost immediately, my compliments. Most others might have tried to stroke the monster or something equally stupid, but this lady knew death.

She picked up the trousers and threw them over. She suddenly attached importance to keeping a safe distance - no idea why.

"You're Philip Eckstein, aren't you?"

I slipped into my much loved Corduroys (I loved them now, before the dog caper I had found them a bit dated), trying to look as professional as possible.

"Some call me Phil. How can I help?"

She tottered restlessly back and forth.

"Could we talk somewhere else?"

I looked surprised.

"Because of the dead dog?"

"Yes, clever clogs", she replied, "because of the dog."

"I can explain, I was attacked..."

"Don't bother," she replied, "How you spend your spare time is your business. I need help urgently. Where can we talk?"

I didn't think twice.

"There's a bar a few doors down. Did you see it?"

"Yes."

"It's a smokers' bar."

"I certainly hope so."

I liked her more and more.

Gino thought a long time about what to call his bar. After months of brooding, while he applied for loans, pounded the pavement for locations and invented cocktail recipes (which he seldom needed), he had a brainwave: *Gino's Bar*. He said he had dithered between that and *Horny Girls Get Free Beer at Gino's Bar*. The bank was against the second one.

It was a great place. I loved it. Imagine a long bar, not dark wood, not glass or chrome, but black lacquered metal with a wooden ledge. Tables, chairs and stools matched. "Low maintenance", Gino explained, "and not intrusively cool. I don't want any media freaks here, highbrows with toilet seat spectacles on their noses." Even though they are clearly the mainstay of Berlin's economy.

The bar was relatively empty, it was a working day and had just turned dark. Two or three local couples were seeing the day out. An elderly regular sat further behind, near the slot machines and raised his beer glass in welcome. I nodded to him and opened the door for my prospective client.

"It's nice here," she purred as I led her to the bar. Gino wasn't around. He was usually the only one on duty at this time.

"Shall I take your jacket?" I asked, she unbuttoned the Caban. I tried hard not to be too obvious but I couldn't wait to see what was hidden under the thick fabric and I was not disappointed.

“Stop staring,” she said, but with a smile that meant “carry on staring but not that way.”

The thin grey sweater fit well and emphasized good, old fashioned femininity. Heidi Klum would have thought her too fat, that’s how feminine she was. Incidentally, the technical term for men who are not into skeletons is “heterosexual”.

I hung the coats on the rack then shuffled over to the bar where her rear already graced one of the stools. I had my cigarettes and lighter with me.

“I could really use one now,” I remarked truthfully. “Do you smoke?”

She looked at the box skeptically.

“It depends. What are they, I've never seen...” She hesitated. “Oh, they're named after you.”

Eckstein No. 5 is not for babies. Okay, babies shouldn't smoke anyway, but you know what I mean. These are really strong. No filter, no silly aromas, they taste like a mixture of asphalt and a house fire. They may not break your smoking habit but do reduce your intake significantly.

You may well ask: Why does Philip Eckstein smoke *Eckstein No 5*? Is the family involved or is he just a stupid bum who finds it stylish? Probably the latter. I don't know if my family had anything to do with the mid-19th century Jewish tobacco factory. *Eckstein* is the oldest existing cigarette brand. I would love to question my family about it, but there are not many of them left, that's because they were all Jewish on my father's side. In Germany.

I don't know what I'm clinging to when I shove an *Eckstein* in my mouth. They taste dreadful, cost too much and are only available on the internet, but they're my first choice. I don't even smoke much, just one or two a day. They're good for me. They make my voice sound gritty and that's useful. I sometimes get interested looks from the ladies who ask themselves what kind of exotic fags they are, that's because of the nifty green box. What sucks is: You can't offer them one, because they then spend the next two hours in the loo.

If you're fed up of your persistent cough and social exclusion but don't want to give up the coolness factor, get yourself these gaspers. They're actually healthy: Believe me, you won't manage more than three a day and you'll instinctively stop lung smoking. The box is really nice, I find the two unicorns amusing (no kidding – it has two unicorns on it!), they are called "Echt & Recht" apparently - the *Eckstein* slogan. The fags themselves are covered in print, very classy; you forget completely that you are poisoning yourself.

"That's right," I replied, and lit up, "we share names. But what's your name?"

She didn't answer immediately, though it really was high time she told me. She sniffed at the tobacco bouquet and decided to risk it.

"Give me one."

It was a sign of courage. Or severe nicotine dependence.

"Okay, but I warn you. Not everyone can stomach them."

"Stop bragging macho man."

She put one between her painted red lips - unfazed by

the missing filter - and I gave her a light. From the corner of my eye I noticed we were being watched – by one of the couples, the old man at the bar and also by Gino, who appeared from the galley.

"Shit, Phil, you should bring along someone like this more often!"

He beamed at my companion and started to play the Italian Casanova. This was evidence of great self-confidence as he was an overweight mid-fifty with the hairstyle of a radiation victim. Gino was of Italian descent, but born in Germany and had no accent, but could imitate it well.

"Buona sera, signorina," he said, unbothered by the smoke we were emitting. "If this guy annoys you, I'll throw him out immediately."

"You and which Orc army?" I grinned. "Would you like a drink?" I had asked the Beauty before Gino appeared.

"Gin and tonic, please," she said, leaving no doubt that I was footing the bill until further notice. Very unfair, it was after all a preliminary interview for a job, not a love affair.

Gino knew my choice and two minutes later I was sipping my Scotch and she her GT. I decided that the big moment had arrived.

"Okay - name and location!"

She smiled wider and pearlier than before.

"Amanda Brecht, Berlin Siemensstadt."

"Delighted to meet you."

Amanda. Not too bad. If it had been more exotic I'd have said she was lying. I usually ask clients for their ID cards but I still had no idea what this was all about. Her whole manner signaled to me that there was a problem, but not so existential that it took the fun out of life. Perhaps the evening would move in the opposite direction? Or in both directions? I had been lucky a couple of times. Taxi drivers claim it happens all the time. Drunken female passengers who don't want to spend the night alone flirt outrageously and voilà - but who knows, maybe they invent such tales to glorify their dreary job. As pastors do.

We put down our drinks.

“What's on your mind, Frau Brecht?”

She stared at the long row of bottles above the bar mirror for a few seconds. I could see she was considering what she could and could not tell me. Which was okay, you rarely got the whole story.

“My brother has disappeared,” she began. “Peter. He's 35, three years older than me. I haven't heard from him for a week now. He's not in his apartment, doesn't answer his phone or cellphone, doesn't respond to emails or text messages.”

“What about the police?”

“I...” She grimaced and nipped at her drink. Then she looked me straight in the eye. “I can't go to the police. It's... I just can't.”

I wasn't born yesterday so I had my suspicions.

“Is he involved in something our uniformed friends shouldn't know about?”

She raised her eyebrows. “Wow. You're good.”

She picked up her *Eckstein* which, like me, she had parked in an ashtray. She inhaled and choked slightly, but kept calm. The exhaled smoke formed a cloud and floated upward. Amanda kept the ciggy in her fingers.

“I'm not certain of everything,” she said, “but I can

piece a lot of it together."

"Then start assembling."

I enjoyed my cigarette and scotch while she put me in the picture.

Peter Brecht had a criminal record. Nothing earth shattering, just a collection of small frauds, smuggling and good old narcotics, but only as a user. Amanda swore he would never ever deal in drugs. She avoided eye contact at this point.

"When was he last in jail?" I asked.

"He was in prison just once, he usually got probation or a fine. But last time the judge lost patience. All he had done was to bring something through customs for a friend. That is to say, he tried."

"And what was it?"

"Caviar."

I hadn't heard that caviar was illegal.

"I didn't hear that caviar was illegal."

Amanda sighed and stubbed out her cigarette. She didn't want another one.

"Beluga, the top quality, earns you 2,500 Euros a kilo apparently. It's a booming business."

She said it with a fervor that seemed suspicious to me. But just then it was unimportant. If she helped her brother with his escapades, that was not my business.

"Sturgeon," she continued, "the fish that produces caviar, can be fished only according to strict regulations. Even so every second can of it on German delicatessen shelves comes from uncontrolled sources. Peter hid just thirty pounds in his car."

"He was small fry," I joked weakly. "How did he get caught?"

"A customs check at the Polish border. They were looking for cigarette smugglers. Really bad luck."

I withheld my opinion. It seemed unlikely that this had been his first smuggling operation. But if you have to wipe out a fish species so rich Westerners have something to smear on their French bread, then so be it. I'm sure fish willingly sacrifice their lives for the honor.

"Peter has been out for a few months and he's really trying to stay clean," declared Amanda, "but he knows so many people, you know."

"Yes, I know."

I really did know. I could start a criminal career anytime, (some of you decent people probably believe I already have one), I certainly know a lot of shady characters. From time to time I get requests like: "This guy owes me five grand, would you rough him up a bit for me" or "Drive this car to Latvia for me, but don't open the trunk." Very amusing. But I must admit that I consider the offers for a few seconds each time. Fortunately I'm usually affluent enough to say no. And as for my "tickets" – they're not that evil now, are they?

"Do you know any of them personally?"

"It depends...," she hesitated.

"Frau Brecht, you don't have to tell me anything. I'll happily look for your brother, but if you don't give me enough information, I may not be able to find him."

She emptied her glass.

"Gino, the same again, please", she gestured towards the bartender chatting to the regulars. It was amazing how easily she addressed him by his first name. I reckoned this was a good opportunity.

"Some call me Phil."

"You've already said that." She smiled benevolently. "Phil."

"Amanda, what do you do for a living?"

"You want to know whether I can afford your services?"

Believe it or not, the fee hadn't crossed my mind yet. I really only wanted to play outboard motor between her breasts. But money is nice too.

"I charge two hundred a day plus expenses," I said, and found again that no other sentence sounded more like Humphrey Bogart.

"I'll pay for the first two days in advance," she said, and picked up the crocodile handbag she had deposited under the stool (it was probably a fake, but so what?). A moment later four hundred Euros slipped into my pocket.

"I'll set out a contract," I said, quite the respectable businessman.

"I trust you, Phil," she assured me. She looked me straight in the eye for a few seconds with an inscrutable gaze that electrified me. "I really do."

I should have made my move here. But because of her missing brother my advances would probably have been unsuccessful. That much I understand about women. At least I had managed to get on familiar first-name terms with her.

"You wanted to tell me what you do for a living."

She didn't bat an eyelid. *Roger that.*

"I'm a nurse. Didn't you notice?"

"Well, your response to the dead pooch was pretty cool, I suppose you see dead bodies every day. And your hands seemed very professional to me. But it doesn't mean..."

She placed her hand on a less intimate place, my upper arm.

"Phil, find my brother for me. If you do, I'll show you where else I'm professional."

I liked her more and more.

We parted with a kiss on the cheek. She kissed me, not I her. She wasn't my mother, damn it. She shifted her shapely derrière out of *Gino's Bar*; its namesake drooled after her as much as I did.

“Seriously, Phil,” he panted, “where did you get that hot piece of ass?”

Men talk that way. I can never get used to it, even less so at this particular moment.

“Take it easy, Gino. She's just a client.”

“Why does it get your back up?”

Good question, why indeed? Change of subject.

“Gino, my old china...”

“Italian. What do you mean, old?” he protested and swigged his beer.

“Gino, you young Italian God,” I took a soft line because I needed a favor off him, “what would you do with a dead dog?”

Gino didn't blink.

“There are animal crematories. Take it there.”

The idea didn't appeal to me. “Do they ask who the animal belongs to?”

Gino didn't reply and kept drinking.

“Gino?”

He put his glass down and lowered his voice.

“Listen, I've been out of it for ages, okay? I want nothing to do with it. I made a bad mistake, I know, so please don't involve me in it.”

Detectives find themselves in these situations sometimes. Your conversation partner suspects you know something although you actually haven't a clue. There are two approaches: you can either let him assume you know so that he keeps talking and betrays himself or just ask outright what the hell he's talking about.

"What the hell are you talking about?"

Gino's eyes narrowed. "What the hell are *you* talking about?"

We stared at each for a while. The old man at the bar wanted more Korn and Gino served him. When he returned, he leaned toward me.

"You've got a dead dog?"

"Yes", I admitted, "in my office."

"And you want to dispose of it as discreetly as possible?"

"Yes."

"So that no one finds it."

"So to speak."

"How did it die?"

"Someone shot him in the head."

"Oh."

Gino looked rather baffled but kept calm. He asked me for an *Eckstein* and we puffed together. This was my third today, and my throat felt raw. A good feeling.

"I know someone who'll get rid of it." Gino said finally.

"Cool. You always know the right people."

"I get around."

"You've never ever left Berlin."

"What for? It's all here. Hookers from around the globe."

"You're a true world citizen," I grinned. "Can you fix it today? No idea how long before a bull terrier starts to stink."

"Okay, I'll call him."

He grabbed his phone and scrolled through a long, long list of contacts. I would have paid millions for that list and so would the police. Someone answered.

"Hello Ramón? It's me... yes, long time no hear, well you know, I'd rather have nothing to do with it anymore. You're not mad at me, are you?... Okay. Listen, could you come over? With your equipment?... A bull terrier... No, it was shot. Self-defense..."

He glanced at me. I nodded.

"Yes, self-defense. I believe so... In an hour? Super... Yes, it will be a real feast for your little pets. Ciao!"

He "hung up". Well, he pressed a button on the keypad. You know. We need a decent expression for it. How about "pressed stop"? Nah. "Switched off"? Could be misunderstood. "Clicked off"?

You are reading this in English – in German it's even worse. The German language just doesn't cater for the needs of the modern age, and we try desperately to cover that up by integrating English words, very often wrongly. For example, there is a pizza delivery service named "Call a Pizza". Doesn't sound like a very sophisticated conversation to me. And we Teutons are the only ones who call their mobile chat gadget a "Handy". The English say "Mobile", the Yanks "Cellphone". No one knows where "Handy" came from.

"Spare me any details," I said to Gino, "but if Ramón wants to know who I am, it might complicate things."

Gino sighed. "Look, Phil, it's like this: In this city - and not just this one - a certain group of people is interested in a certain type of entertainment."

"What entertainment? Karaoke? Ballet? Kabuki theatre?"

"Dog fights."

What an interesting evening.

"Really?" I said. "In Berlin?"

"Cologne is the German Mecca. But there are so many dogs in Berlin it's easy to find supplies here."

Indeed. There are far too many dogs in Berlin. I have nothing against these artificially created species, bred from foxes and wolves for the needs of mankind, but I don't want to be a dog owner. What are dog owners? People who go about collecting shit.

At least they should do, but don't. Take a look at Berlin.

"I was involved in it for a while," Gino admitted embarrassed. "I got fed up pretty quickly. I don't particularly like dogs, but this was just sadism. Have you ever seen a Doberman bite off the nose of an Alsatian?"

"No, you don't see that stuff on TV."

"Or a Mastiff snatch at the genitals of an Irish Setter?"

"Fascinating, but I think I could live without that."

"Me too."

I'd had enough tobacco and alcohol for today, the pain had almost gone. It would twinge for a few days but I could deal with that. I ordered a soda while Gino served the various guests who now drifted in. As a smokers' bar, *Gino's* was highly sought after, even though it was uncertain how long the privilege would last. Eventually there'd be nowhere to smoke anymore, but I had to admit I found that preferable. One should, of course, have a choice, but I didn't like the idea that waiters and bartenders exposed themselves to a cancer risk just to have a job. Construction workers had to wear helmets, and I could enjoy being miserable even without a cigarette.

Things were a bit strained when Ramón appeared because I was a stranger to him and what he was doing was illegal, an atrocity of apocalyptic dimensions and the end of civilization as we know it. He was a muscle-bound, toned and tattooed gentleman of Hispanic origin who, with very little effort, could have beaten me to death with an iron chain. I should mention that he wore an iron chain around his neck.

Gino vouched for my discretion and I proved my generosity with a hundred Euro note. We trudged up to my office where Ramón inspected the carcass. He was delighted.

"Huge, plenty of meat, at least fifty pounds," he muttered with a slight accent. He'd obviously been in Germany for some time.

He took a large, sturdy plastic bag out of his gym bag.

"You're not going to eat it, are you?"

Oh man, I'm not a political correctness devotee, but that was really racist. Ramón looked at me with contempt inappropriate for a professional animal abuser.

"I give it to my dogs," he said quietly. "Lots of protein, bull terrier. And the strength and killer instinct is passed on to them. Was it aggressive?"

"Shit, yes, a fucking psychopath." I was about to show him my leg, but restrained myself in time. I think I was a bit drunk. I must restrict my Scotch intake.

I helped Ramón to stuff Fausto into the bag. He needed no help carrying the dog downstairs; he just slung the bag over his shoulder. We said goodbye in the street where his Range Rover was parked and I went back upstairs.

I cleared up a bit in the office, cleaned the gun carefully, grabbed my notebook and left. My apartment was on the floor above, a luxury that I really appreciate.

It had been a tough day, full of nasty goings-on but also with a wonderful encounter with a remarkable woman. I knew Amanda was unique. Some women just have that *je ne sais quoi*, as the Egyptians say. If you look around you'll see that lots of women have exciting bodies but then have something that spoils them, like stained teeth (my personal no-go) or the personality of a Bulgarian hedge witch.

I got into my bed for a change. I often nod off on the couch which is no good for my back. I keep myself fit at the local gym but I still have to be careful. For a while I considered what I might find unlikable about Amanda. I hadn't had time to analyze her in detail and it would have to be delayed for a while because we had an appointment at her brother's flat tomorrow morning.

There were a couple of strange things. She seemed to be pretty well heeled for a nurse. Well, it was all about her brother. She was probably in cahoots with him and as a result she was afraid of the police. It was perfectly clear that she knew more than she admitted. She was worried about her brother, but set a limit if it meant trouble for her. We matched perfectly.

I slept the sleep of the just or, should I say, the ill-treated. Things could only get better, I thought. The truth was that, in comparison with what was to come, the day had been a picnic.

Trace to Tempelhof

Peter Brecht's flat was in Prenzlauer Berg. I thought that was pretty amazing, petty criminals usually preferred cheaper areas such as Wedding or Lichtenberg. That's not where they carry out their evil deeds though as there are too few potential victims but quite a few fences and some good hiding places. Infrastructure is as important for criminals as it is for families with children, small businesses and prostitutes.

"Prenzlberg" has a problem: The East German ghetto, formerly full of the maladjusted marginalized, had been reinvented, it now looked really good and was populated by nice people with good jobs and children. This understandably filled countless other Berliners with hate and fury and they did everything to ensure that this disaster was not repeated in Kreuzberg or Friedrichshain. A risk which did not really exist. Why people were eager to live in grubby Kreuzberg was beyond me.

Amanda greeted me at the front door of the old building. She was wearing the same clothes as yesterday but I would have recognized her even in a bin bag. The weather had improved, the sun was shining and I was already perspiring.

"Phil, hi! I was afraid you might not turn up!"

"Why not? You paid me and I'm buyable."

She kissed me on the cheek again and, maybe I imagined it, she was about four millimeters closer to my mouth than yesterday. It took a superhuman effort not to put my hand on her haunch, but it was damn early morning and the matter in hand was serious.

"I haven't got a key," she said, as we climbed up the

stairs (a friendly/stupid neighbor had opened the main door), “is that a problem?”

“Not at all,” I assured her, hoping I sounded really cool. As we reached the door with “Brecht” on it, I took out my tool pouch, which I called my “Detlev-purse” just like my old man. This one contained a set of completely different tools.

I opted for a simple titan lock picker, firm but flexible. It took six seconds. The door was closed but not locked.

Amanda was impressed and clapped her hands.

“You're a true professional.”

I pretended not to care that she found me great and we entered the apartment. I restrained her.

“How do you know he's not in his flat?”

She looked at me surprised.

“Well, I've rung the bell and knocked repeatedly for three days running and nothing has happened.”

I made a face which was probably a bit too pessimistic. It dawned on her.

“You think he could be ..?”

“...lying here dead, in his own vomit? Yes, he could be.”

I need to work on my tactfulness. That was a good example. I love women, but I'm not like them and they realize that pretty quickly. Did I mention that I've never had a long term relationship? That's how things will stay.

Amanda stood by the door while I looked around. It took two minutes to establish there was no dead body. That was good because it would have distressed Amanda, but bad because I had to continue the assignment for no extra money. “It's okay, Amanda”, I called out, “there's no one here.”

She closed the door and joined me with a distant expression in her eyes but relief on her face. If this story were to be filmed, we'd need a first-class actress for her role. Could she be one herself?

“Well”, she asked, “what now?”

“When were you last here?”

“Over a week ago.”

“Has anything changed here?”

She looked around carefully and shook her head. It was a standard room with a bed, TV cabinet, a round dining table, chairs, a wardrobe and coffee table all from Ikea. The latter, I found most interesting, because it was full of stuff whereas everything else was empty. There were DVDs in the cupboard and some mens' magazines with a lot of sex, violence and ball kicking. A team pennant and poster showed he was a fan of an obscure football club called “Hertha BSC”. Probably in the third division by now.

There was some interesting stuff on the coffee table, however: a brown envelope, an A4 notepad (full of scribbles) and a key. I sat on the couch and examined them, while Amanda checked the bathroom and kitchen for clues.

“Fix me a coffee while you're there,” I called out and she laughed briefly, but a few minutes later I heard the coffee machine gurgling. Women love fussing over men and as a nurse she couldn't withstand.

To my delight, the envelope contained exactly what a detective needs: Photos. They were digital but printed on photo paper. Nothing intimate, just pretty boring stuff, mainly sites, as if someone was taking photographs of movie locations to show to the director.

City streets. Unidentifiable country roads, the photos pictured a route through totally deserted areas. A rat run for smugglers perhaps.

Buildings. Probably empty, run down factories or office buildings. That was interesting; a few struck me as familiar. I know Berlin very well, especially the dilapidated bits, and these images were made for the 2014 "Berlin is a shit hole"- Calendar.

A few photos appeared to have been made for fun: A few animals, a few places of interest, nothing unusual. I checked the buildings again when Amanda handed me a cup of coffee and sat down beside me.

"Found anything?"

I showed her the pictures.

"Do they mean anything to you?"

She looked through them but only shrugged her shoulders.

"I don't recognize anything apart from *Goldelse* and the *Konzerthaus*."

I was examining a picture of a factory site. I looked closer.

"There, in the background... that's the gasometer in Schöneberg," I explained. "Just about a mile away."

"Then it's near Südkreuz" said Amanda who was equally knowledgeable about Berlin. "Why on earth did he photograph all this stuff?"

"Maybe someone else did it. The envelope didn't come by mail, there's nothing on it, but someone may have given him the pictures as a guide."

We looked through the pictures again but could only identify the factory.

I turned to the notepad. Peter Brecht had scrawled a

few numbers and doodles, nothing revealing. They included a large penis with testicles he had drawn. Let's face it, all men do that. It has nothing to do with being gay, it's just fun. I think. If a woman did it, it would be a good reason to marry her. Maybe they do draw them. I must check out a few ladies' loos when I get the chance.

A date, eight days ago, and time were more interesting and filled Amanda with turmoil. She looked at me anxiously, as if she wanted to hear a soothing phrase like "it's pure coincidence" or "it means nothing." But I'm not the comforter type. I have already mentioned that I've never had a long term relationship, haven't I?

Below the date were the abbreviation "KFW" and the word "canteen". Then it clicked.

"The Karl Friedrich Werke", I muttered, "whereabouts are they? In Tempelhof?"

"The escalator manufacturer?" Amanda had heard of it. After the war KFW had been a key growth factor in Berlin. Eventually, however, they were swallowed by Thyssen and, like everything else, relocated, away from the unsafe Diaspora, to cozy West Germany. I wasn't born in Berlin, but it riles me that those who profited most from the division of Germany by getting a free delivery of huge companies such as Allianz, Commerzbank, Deutsche Bank, Dresdner Bank, Daimler-Benz and most of Siemens, now gripe about Berlin's parasitism. Well, dear Hessians, we'll forget the equalization payments as soon as you return our banks to us, oh, and the tax revenue for the last sixty years. Agreed? You just keep paying and are thankful you're in a position to do so.

"We can soon find out," I thought. "Does your brother own a computer?"

“Well, an iPad”, Amanda said, “shall I see if I can find it?”

We searched together. I hoped to find, firstly, other clues and, secondly, the location of the former KFW on the Internet. It was quite embarrassing, it seemed I'd have to invest in an iPad, even a smartphone was obviously no longer adequate.

“Nothing,” Amanda summed up, after we finished our search. “He must have taken it with him.”

“No problem,” I said, and put the photos, notepad and keys in the envelope. “We'll go to an internet café.”

Amanda looked at her watch.

“Sorry, I can't. I have to go to work. Someone has been standing in for me for the last few days but she can't anymore. You'll have to do it alone, Phil.”

I hope my disappointment didn't show. We said goodbye in front of the house (two kisses on the cheek, one of them near my non-existent mustache), she got into her Peugeot and I into my Astra

Yes, Astra. What about it? Investigators must be inconspicuous. I wore inconspicuous clothing, was an average looking guy (that’s easy in Germany) and I drove an Astra. I have observed and shadowed people in that jalopy and never attracted attention. Try that in an Aston Martin or BMW convertible. The Opel emblem also reminded me of home. Bochum, I’m fond of you...

Is Opel still in Bochum when you read this, I wonder?

The remains of the Karl Friedrich Werke stood in the no man's land between Tempelhof and Schöneberg. I drove around a bit before finding the access road and did the remaining half mile on foot. There was still some industry, trade and even allotments there but, for the most part, it was abandoned, decayed and overrun with weeds.

I had the photos with me and compared them with the surroundings. It seemed some were intended as signposts. Neither my ADAC map nor my satnav were precise enough to find the place so it made sense. There was a picture of wasteland with a single tree on it that was very distinctive – clearly a pointer.

I wondered what I would find. If these photos were there to show Peter Brecht where to go he would have taken them with him. But maybe he had made the pictures to give to someone else. Whatever. As a detective you have to piece things together. I was paid per day not per detected brother.

I came to a three-meter high steel fence that bordered the KFW. Behind it was a large, gutted hall with three floors. I could see straight through it, but some areas were hidden from the eye. The door was locked.

The key fit. I could've picked it open, but it's nicer to be able to avoid that hassle. Then again, if the key was in Brecht's apartment - how likely was it that he was around?

I was pretty keyed up. Did you ever go into abandoned houses or properties just to look around as a child? It's exciting, even though you're looking for a pot of gold or a secret door that leads to a fantasy world and not a person. Curiously, it was less fun with a friend than if you were alone. The sense of danger was much more intense. I think I was more than just excited, I was actually a little scared. If anything happened to me here, there was no one to help me.

The ground floor had obviously been the main production hall and was half the height of the whole building, twice as high as the other two floors. The KFW had made escalators for half of Germany in its glory days, with manufacturing facilities not just here but also in Hamburg and Munich - wherever escalators were needed. They had taken the machines and production lines with them, only crane rails and rusty scaffolding testified to their earlier activities. Now nothing of interest was left.

Suddenly I jumped.

What was that?

The sound was hard to define, sort of metallic. It came from upstairs.

Brecht's note had said “Canteen”. I reckoned it was on the first floor and I was right. After carefully clambering up a crumbling, partially collapsed stairway, I opened a broken door and found myself in a sunlit hall, where two hundred people used to eat lunch. There were still a few tables left.

And rats.

I could see as many as seven, there must be a rat's nest somewhere. Delightful. For a moment I considered using my gun, but realized it was silly as the critters scuttled away as soon as I walked into the hall.

This looked like a dead end, I had to admit. There was no evidence that anyone had been here recently. Dust everywhere and where there was no dust there was dirt of all kinds. I resolved to brush my shoes thoroughly that evening. Rats and mice transmit the Hanta virus, amongst other things.

There was another door further down, probably the former kitchen. It had a large hatch through which I could see some broken cabinets. The door was ajar; a quick look wouldn't hurt.

Did I behave stupidly that day?

Should I have pulled my gun? What for, there was no one there, I could have shot at something just for fun but I only do that at shooting practice. I had no reason to assume this was a dangerous situation.

But the key fit.

Silly me.

No, don't comfort me. I was stupid and reckless. Isn't this what guns are for?

The kitchen was the size of a classroom with cabinets, a couple of taps and a tiled white floor.

Peter Brecht's corpse lay flat on its back in a pool of dried blood.

I froze; for a moment I lost my concentration. It was a long moment. Someone had been lurking there and he didn't mess about. A hard blow to the back of my head knocked me to the floor.

I remember thinking: *The first corpse. About time.*

And then: *Ooowwwwww!!!*

Lisa Becker

Every self-respecting detective should wake up next to a corpse at least once in a lifetime.

Well, I've got that sorted.

I checked my watch and saw I had been unconscious for about twenty minutes. Peter Brecht was still there, still dead and had been for days. He wasn't bored, the flies and worms saw to that, and that was just the beginning.

Yours truly got up and had a bunch of questions. For instance, why wasn't I dead? My bold conclusion, on seeing the gaping wound in Brecht's chest, was that someone had been killed here but whoever had done it did not necessarily want to bump off anyone else. My good luck, but somehow unprofessional. What type of killers were they?

How badly was I injured? A brief inspection in half a mirror on the wall displayed a nasty bruise and a neck like an American Redneck. I wiped myself down quickly. I went through my pockets, still a bit shaky. Everything was there: wallet, money, plastic money... and my Walther! They hadn't even taken my gun. That was somehow embarrassing.

Who did I mean by “they”? “They” could be anyone from a gang of Russian Mafiosowskis to a deranged tramp. No, a tramp would have taken my money. And the Russians my gun. Whoever I had stumbled upon was not in the least interested in me. They hadn't even searched me. They had finished, or failed in, whatever they were doing, which meant there was no more reason for me to be here.

There was nothing in the dead brother's pockets. Even though I didn't have a smartphone, I had the advantage of a mobile phone that could take pictures, so I photographed the corpse and the rest of the crime scene.

I'd have to show Amanda the pictures; I wasn't exactly looking forward to it. Highly unlikely that she'd be interested in sex after that. Although it is sometimes said that death is an aphrodisiac. For an animal a dead companion means: These are dangerous times, make more babies! But I doubted it would work with Amanda.

What would?

I know it's outrageous to say it, but honestly, between you and me, this man meant nothing to me. A habitual criminal who had become involved with the wrong people, he had only himself to blame. If Fatso and his pooch had made mincemeat out of me I would've said: It was your own fault, Phil.

The next thing I had to do with the phone was to inform the police. Unquestionably. In this country we live according to the rule of law and I wasn't an avenging angel. A murder had to be reported.

"Could I please speak to Kommissarin Becker?"

Lisa Becker was the rising star in homicide, this year alone she had, along with her much too good-looking partner, contributed significantly to the apprehension of two serial killers. The lucky bastard bedded her regularly. Lisa was plump with curves that put the hairpin bends in Tuscany in the shade. She was also very smart, funny and not an inhibited office bimbo.

"What's up, Phil?"

"I just woke up next to a corpse."

"Great!" she cheered. "Congratulations, you always

wanted to do that!"

See what I mean?

"Seriously, Lisa."

"Oh. Where are you?"

"Do you know the old KFW building?"

I gave directions and explained the situation as best I could. In thirty minutes the entire force would be here, forensics, forensic medicine, the lot. I thought it unlikely they would find anything interesting except, of course, my fingerprints. Those are taken when you apply for a gun.

Now I could look around the place myself even though I felt no great desire to do so. My job was done, I had found Peter Brecht. The search for his murderer was not in my remit.

You could now say: "But the book hasn't ended yet!"

Well spotted.

"You know nothing?"

Lisa Becker pouted. She was so cute; she sometimes played the obstinate little girl to hide what she was really thinking. We talked outside in the KFW parking lot. It was more of an interrogation from her perspective but she didn't show it. We knew and, I hoped, liked each other - she wouldn't mess me around.

"I've no idea who shot him," I insisted. "I don't know who put the Ouchy on my head, neither do I know if it was the same person. I know as little about the background as my client does. No idea what Brecht was doing here."

"You're a great detective."

"Well, I found him after just three hours of work.

That's not bad at all."

"Who's your client?"

"His sister, Amanda."

"I'd like a word with her."

I gave her the mobile number.

"Would you like to tell her?" Lisa asked.

I groaned inwardly. And outwardly.

"Come on," grumbled Lisa, "that's what she's paying you for. I can think of nicer things to do."

"So can I."

"Yeah, but you're an emotionally crippled piece of shit," said Lisa, "My job hasn't made me so callous yet."

"All the more reason for you..."

"Fraidy cat..."

"Okay!" I gave in.

Lisa accompanied me for a part of the way.

"That was a bit much the other day," she said out of the blue.

"What?"

"That businessman pervert", she said innocently, "with the photos in the *Kurier*."

"What's it got to do with me?" Honestly. I'm taken in every time. Breasts have too powerful an influence on me and the way Lisa wore her blouse was very spectator-friendly.

She grinned at me triumphantly.

"A colleague told me a complaint had been lodged against the owner of the hotel where the guy committed his misdeeds. For some reason the guy wants revenge on the hotel, not the photographer. Invasion of privacy and so on. It'll get him nowhere, but my colleague is convinced that someone got access to that particular room, which doesn't belong to the hotel. Some sleazy little wretch of a private eye who has made a career of his addiction to watching people having sex. That type of person."

"Yes, absolutely revolting," I agreed. "What made you think of me?"

"The camera had gone, but a maid told my colleague that an air conditioning mechanic had been in there and he had smoked some vile weed in a strange, green cigarette box on the balcony."

"Interesting."

"Yes, any idea why the guy didn't charge the snoop? He would have had a much greater chance of success. It's a fair question, isn't it?"

"Perhaps he didn't know who it was."

"His future ex-wife could have told him," Lisa speculated.

I threw all my years of experience in terms of human knowledge and reading of facial expression into interpreting whether Lisa's expression indicated whether they knew anything about the "parking ticket". It seemed unlikely, but the colleague's investigation had taken place before today, that is, it took place before I screwed the fat guy. He had kept it private for sure, in order not to incriminate himself. And he was about to turn me into blood-and-bone stew. I was safe.

I left Lisa after calling Amanda under her eagle eye. I hadn't handed over the photos and was sparing with information. I had an obligation to keep my client out of trouble. That was my credo, although there are no rules as such. In point of fact I wanted to talk to her before I gave the buxom Kommissar any information.

I neither had Amanda's address nor did I know in which hospital she worked, but she said she would come to my office immediately.

“I'm testing matron's patience to the limit,” she lamented, and settled on the couch. “Have you found him?”

I had never delivered bad news before and hadn't the faintest idea how to do it. Lisa had very cleverly passed the buck, it was clearly her duty. Damn those magnificent boobs!

I told Amanda in a few words what had happened. I didn't get as far as the blow on the back of my head.

Many, very many women have wept in my office. Deceived wives, mainly. Sometimes I make women cry just for the fun of it. Does that make me a bad person? Yes, I suppose it does.

Amanda didn't cry out or weep, not even when I showed her the cell phone photos on the laptop. For a moment I thought it wasn't Peter, but she confirmed his identity.

I offered her a cigarette and she sucked at the *Eckstein* like a vacuum cleaner. She said nothing. Neither did I. For about ten minutes.

“The police will call you soon,” I told her, “I know the senior investigator. She's very good.”

She looked at me with a strange expression. “You've given the cops my cell phone number?”

“I had to explain what I was doing there,” I defended myself, “otherwise I would have been blamed.”

“I can't afford that. That’s why I came to you.”

“You don't have to tell them anything. Just identify

him, that's all. Of course..."

"What?"

"Well, if you want to know who eradicated your brother, then you have to give them some information. The Kommissar is good, but at the moment she has only a body to go on, nothing else."

"What else did you tell them?"

"That you asked me to look for him and that I had evidence about the KFW. The photos I kept to myself."

"Good."

She got up and took a cigarette from the pack on the desk. I meekly gave her a light.

"Not that good," I took the cue, "the police can achieve much more with the pictures than we can, they have manpower and equipment. I don't know how deeply involved you are but I suggest that you cooperate with them. Otherwise you could be in the line of fire."

She glared at me. God, she was pure erotic even when she was angry.

"What are you talking about? I'm not a criminal!"

I left it at that.

She sank back onto the couch and signaled to me with the cigarette-free hand to join her. I did, with great joy and enthusiasm.

She put her cigarette into the ashtray on the coffee table and crossed her legs. She was wearing jeans, not a frock, otherwise it would have been ripe for an Oscar, well maybe just a Golden Camera.

"Phil, I'm frightened." She looked me in the eye and my stomach tightened. Was it sympathy or just flatulence.

"I'll be frank: My brother and I, we got on all right, but

we weren't bosom buddies. He often misled me; he used to borrow money which I never saw again. I'm sorry he's dead and I wish I could have helped him, but he got involved with people he couldn't handle. It was his own fault. That's why I can't cry."

"You don't have to justify yourself. I haven't cried since I was four."

"He told me hardly anything," she ignored me. "But he and others were planning to smuggle something into the country. Not caviar, something really valuable. In a suitcase. That's all I know."

"Any clues about the masterminds?" I asked. "If so, go to the police. Lisa Becker will be fair with you."

"I'm not afraid of the pigs."

"You know, the more you say 'pigs', the lower your credibility falls," I remarked. "I haven't yet asked if you've been in jail."

"No, I haven't" she replied, still smiling. It was quite scary.

"I realize that I know very little about you. Where you live, where you work, your whole background."

"I don't pay you to spy on me, sweetheart," she cooed and her foot wandered up my calf.

"You obviously have something to hide," I replied, concealing my tension, "and I respect that. I suggest we go our separate ways now. I've delivered the goods in a single day. If you like, I'll give you two hundred back."

She bit her lip and stared out the window. She then picked up her cigarette and produced a few smoke rings.

"Phil, when I say I'm frightened I don't mean of our beloved law enforcers," she said. "I'm afraid of the 'masterminds' as you call them."

"But if you knew nothing about the deal..."

"But they don't know that, do they?"

"Talk to the police. They can protect you."

"Oh, really? Even though I have nothing to offer, no information at all? Even if your little friend were on my side, it wouldn't guarantee anything."

I had to smile inwardly, no one who knew Lisa would call her "little". But Amanda was right, of course.

"What will you do? Go underground?" I suggested. "I could help you with that."

"That would be the last resort," she said and stubbed out her ciggy. "When all other options have been exhausted."

"And what options do you have?"

She leaned towards me. Suddenly her face was so close to mine I could smell the cigarette bouquet. On her it was more like *Chanel No. 5* than *Eckstein No. 5*

"You're the detective. Find out who's behind all this. If you do that, I can go to the police. Or have a chat with them, so they leave me alone. No idea which would be more helpful. Right now I need more information, then I'd have more options. Anyway, I don't want to start a completely new life unless it's absolutely necessary. I need you, Phil."

Her fingers slid onto my neck and my hair stood on end like... well, you know. I had to do something with my hands, so they landed on her thigh. Then on her hips. No resistance. I didn't want to go any further because of her dead brother. She seemed to be of the same mind and moved away a few millimeters to mark the border.

The kiss was of course inevitable.

The cigarette didn't spoil it at all. I was used to that. It was definitely the best damn bowel-twisting kiss I had ever experienced. She nibbled at my lower lip, licked my mouth, fondled my hair, the whole works. I grabbed her soft, yielding body and pressed it against me where I wanted it. I stopped there because she was the aggressor, she defined the rules. And the game was over in ten seconds.

Her cell phone rang, and we both knew it had to be answered.

“Hello?... Yes, I am... Herr Eckstein told me... Thank you... Yes, it's him, I recognized him in the pictures Herr Eckstein made...”

They blathered for a few minutes. When she hung up, I looked at her searchingly.

“Are you planning to see them?”

She shrugged her shoulders.

“No. I told them it was my brother. I've no obligation to do more than that, right?”

“That won't satisfy them.”

“My brother has been murdered and I'm now supposed to undergo interrogation?”

“If you don't it'll arouse suspicion.”

“Whose? Yours or that of your beloved cop bitch?”

The mood had cooled considerably. I would have thrown her out normally, but something held me back. Her face. I was shocked at how incredibly sad she looked, how desperate and afraid. An actress casting for her part would need to have won at least two Oscars even before she was allowed to audition.

I did what men are supposed to do in such situations: I put my arms around her. She resisted at first, but then dropped the mask of the callous lone fighter, she really needed me. I swear I didn't even get a hard-on. She clung to me and cried on my shoulder for a while.

"I'm all alone now," she whispered almost inaudibly. "It's all too much."

I held her tight and it felt really good. I wasn't used to the protector role, the hero. Nobody had ever told me about it. So that's why so many people care for others, share their emotions, support them. It's a great feeling. I wanted more.

We slowly parted and she kissed me, very caringly this time, as if not to scare me off.

"Please say that you'll help me. Please, Phil."

"I will help you, Amanda," I answered obediently. "You can rely on me."

"I shall have to hide," she reflected, "from the police, from these other people..."

"Stay here," I suggested, and honestly, I was not at that moment thinking what you're thinking. "My apartment is upstairs. I can sleep on the couch."

She looked at me, and I was delighted to see the impish smile and challenging gaze again.

"If you're on the couch and I'm in your bed, how will you screw me?"

Good point.

You'd like to hear details, am I right? Well, gentlemen hold their tongues and enjoy. That's what *gentlemen* do.

Amanda was her usual self in bed: Self-confident, demanding, aggressive, but all woman at the right moment. She took the active part out of concern for my recent leg and head injuries, I highly recommend this to any Macho, who says he has to "give it" to the ladies. Amanda was different: She wanted both of us to be satisfied and since my satisfaction was a mere formality and she knew best what made her mailbox ring (I'll have to reword that phrase, I think), she threw me on my back and mounted me as if she were changing Pony Express horses at full gallop. Her large, soft breasts slapped gently so near my face I could suck them like a half-starved bison calf. She sensed instinctively when to change the tempo or rhythm, so the whole performance was not over in a jiffy, it lasted over an hour. Towards the end, she gripped my shoulders, clenched her teeth and let out a sound deceptively like a Jaguar who has just caught his lady in the bushes with his best pal.

You could say: Eckstein, there were plenty of animals in that description, old man, that strikes me as odd – but that's because it was somehow animalistic. I'm a lover of women and their visual stimuli, sex was never really a big thing for me. I sometimes think the most exciting part is the moment when a woman unclasps her bra. Everything else is plain drudgery.

Amanda didn't complain about the effort. She was perspiring, but not sweating. With a happy, but triumphant laugh she dismounted and stretched out on the bed next to me. We had used a condom, I now disposed of it efficiently by tying a knot and throwing it into a corner. She watched me fascinated and giggled even more.

"You're a funny old thing, Philip Eckstein."

"Thing? Don't you mean 'stallion' or 'bull'?"

"Okay: you're a funny old stallion, Philip Eckstein."

"Thank you."

We didn't go to sleep because it was still broad daylight. The sun shone faintly, the sky was cloudy and I could hear the neighbors talking in the yard. It was quite likely that they had heard us.

We spoke very little. She talked about her brother. They got on well as children but he went slowly off the rails. She had to help provide false alibis, lend him money and so forth. She preferred not to say too much, I could tell. Having sex didn't mean that we trusted each other.

But we gradually returned to the theme of the day.

"You must know at least a couple of his regular mates," I insisted, "with those, we could find out even more."

"I'm thinking about it," she replied and took the cigarette we were sharing out of my hand. "Yes, I know a couple of guys. Just regular guys, you know, like Peter once was. One was called Uwe, one Mustafa and another Pyotr. I wanted nothing to do with them. They flirted with me all the time and Peter just grinned, the bastard."

"Don't you have more than their first names? There was no address book in the apartment or in his..."

I stopped in time. She mustn't feel immoral because she was lying naked next to the man who had found her brother's body earlier that day. But she wasn't listening, she was thinking.

"I think his contacts were on his iPad and his cell phone. They've both vanished?"

"Yes."

"Then I'm at a loss. Shall we rummage through his apartment again?"

"We can't get in anymore. The apartment has been searched and sealed. Before you ask: I refuse go to jail for you by breaking into a sealed apartment. I draw the line there."

"All right," she smiled and put the *Eckstein* in my mouth. "I wouldn't expect that. But then I really don't know what to do."

"What about venues? Did Peter and his pals have a favorite bar?"

"Oh." She was silent for a moment, then she beamed at me. "Yes, a strip club, the Blue Flamingo!"

"I know that one," I said, just a bit too fast. Her gaze was direct. "A Berlin private eye has to know places like that. It's pretty notorious."

"Notorious for what? For strange stains on the seat cushions?"

"Yes, that, and for being one of the main bases of what is left of organized crime not led by biker gangs or Arab-Turkish extended families. The *Blue Flamingo* belongs to Hartmut Kropf apparently."

"Who's that?"

"He's also known as ‚the lawn mower'."

"A hobby gardener?"

"It has more to do with the way he treats competitors and other opponents when he is tired of their existence."

"Oh shit." She was pale. Her face was, her breasts kept their healthy color.

“They're just rumors,” I reassured her (and me). “Gangsters spread them to earn respect.”

“It works perfectly, but where does that leave us?”

I made a decision.

“I shall go there tonight and check things out.”

“Is that wise?” She sat up and looked at me anxiously. I watched her nipples erect. It seemed that for her danger was the great aphrodisiac, not death. “I don't want anything to happen to you. Not again. You've been badly messed up in the last twenty-four hours.”

“I'm okay,” I assured her and it was true. This woman awakened my senses better than any Scotch or roller coaster ride. I stubbed out the cigarette in the ashtray on the bedside table. “Leave it to me.”

“Should I stay here?”

Good question. Nothing had been taken while I was unconscious but it was likely that our enemies knew who I was.

“I'll take you to Gino later,” I decided. “I trust him and he'll eat out of your hand.”

“Yuck.”

“He's a very nice guy in his own special, unique way, it takes just a couple of years to learn to appreciate him.”

The dog fights I put to one side as I did with other things. Suddenly I wasn't so sure that it was a good idea. But at this point it wasn't possible to avoid risks. I was dealing with an unknown enemy and he was a few steps ahead of me.

Perhaps you've been to one of these exclusive businessmen strip clubs where ladies perform lascivious dances in private rooms with their own small stage in front of the noses (and other organs) of male guests. They use electronic music, not hard techno, just a melancholy soundscape, it's called Trance, I believe, but, to be honest, the music is unimportant. It's about giving clients the illusion that they are not in a strip joint getting horny ogling naked women but in a super cool setting, pursuing a trendy urban lifestyle - as evidenced by the fact that you pay 28 Euros for a drink.

The *Blue Flamingo* on Boxhagener Strasse in Friedrichshain was nothing like that. There was a stage with a catwalk and three aluminum poles. The room was decorated in red and gold and filled with men of different age groups, sometimes alone, sometimes in groups, sitting at small tables. They were celebrating stag or birthday parties, even early prison releases or divorces. It was an atmosphere of fun, alcohol and shame.

Shame? Yes, of course. Men don't really want to watch a striptease. They are unpleasantly aware that the bodies that gratify them in books, videos and on *porn.com* belong to real human beings. And these humans here were able to see you!

Every man wants the object of his desire to like or at least respect him, or better still to desire him sexually. This is ruled out completely if the man pays for her to strip or have sex with him. Nothing makes a man less attractive than the knowledge that he has to pay for sex or nudity. No woman with an ounce of self-respect would surrender to someone like that voluntarily. Only if he paid. And so we come full circle.

I've never paid for sex. My sacred oath is that when the time comes when no woman wants to look at my naked, old, flabby and liver-spotted body, I will terminate my sex life and devote myself to other things. I might become a photographer, like Bryan Adams.

I wasn't as familiar with The *Blue Flamingo* as with other similar establishments. They depressed me, I didn't enjoy going there, but in my line of work it's necessary to maintain certain contacts.

"Hi," the bouncer welcomed me. It was eleven o'clock, the right time to visit a night club. It was raining and he didn't fuss around, he just let me in. "Nothing doing," he said, well it was Tuesday, he then frisked me discreetly for weapons or whatever. Once inside I handed over my coat at the cloakroom and headed for the bar. There was just one girl on stage, a bit pale, but pretty and shapely. Single guests sat at four separate tables and watched her with uneasy smiles as they slurped their overpriced bubbly. The music was subtle disco music which could be ignored. It was still pretty early.

The bartender was a woman, a good example of a working class landlady and lusted after by every man in the depths of his soul: Ample, devilish boobs and bedroom eyes, but unfortunately already about 62 years old.

"What'll it be, stranger," she asked, and batted her heavily painted eyelids. I liked her, she was playing saloon hostess. I marveled at her crater-deep neckline and ordered a scotch and Schweppes. I prefer it neat but I needed to keep a clear head.

"May I smoke here," I asked, as she brought my drink. The rules changed constantly.

"Sorry, not at the moment," she said, "we've been cautioned a couple of times already and now have to behave."

I found it hard to believe that Hartmut "lawn mower" Kropf cared much about what Health and Safety had to say. On the other hand they had put Al Capone behind bars for tax evasion.

I didn't have a grand plan. Sometimes one must follow an impulse. The impulse came when two guys, obviously regulars, came in. The girl at the door greeted them with cheeks kisses, one gave her a firm pat on the butt which she acknowledged with a fake chuckle.

The two walked straight to the bar and sat opposite me. The hostess, whom I secretly baptized Olga, gave them their drinks without being told. Pure vodka. A narcotic almost as efficient as beloved herbal tonic Klosterfrau Melissengeist (which had 80 % plus alcohol), more than suitable for a relaxing evening. I suspected they had an appointment.

They chatted quietly about this and that and I waited for an opportunity to join in.

"I now believe the airport will never be completed," the wiry guy in the gray suit grinned. He had white-blond hair so it was difficult to determine his age, fortyish probably.

"In a few years it will all be forgotten," his friend retorted, he was about the same age, a type that many would, at first glance, call fatty. Despite the wide beige jacket and wide jeans I could see he wasn't. He was muscle-bound, like a gorilla, and not very tall. I wouldn't mess with him, even though he was two heads shorter than me.

They chatted for a while about the Berlin-Brandenburg Airport, whose opening had been delayed again. This was normal for construction projects and to be expected with such a large one. Every Berliner fancied himself to be an expert in the field of airport construction and competent to voice an opinion on it. I found it amusing that even two obvious crooks had fallen victim to the virus. We believe that they are different to normal citizens but even they have to kill time somehow. Criminals don't work long hours, that's one of the benefits. If you had to burgle, cheat, mug and do people in all day, you might just as well become bank clerk.

"The airport? It'll be complete when airport taxes have made flights unaffordable for ordinary mortals," I muttered in their direction.

I'm bad at small talk when it comes to men, I must admit. With women I'm motivated because I want to subtly bring into play a theoretical future perspective of sexual intercourse with me. I can't chat to men or rather, men can't chat to me.

The bullshit men talk!

"*It's easy: Chuck the Greeks out of Euroland, they can flog their islands and pay their debts!*"

"*Ban the burka, then they'll all go back to where they came from!*"

"*When Cologne is back in Bundesliga, they're well on their way to the Champions League!*"

And these people are entitled to the vote.

The wiry guy grinned at my remark about the airport.

"That's what I think," he said, "but never mind. We'll have raked in a profit by then."

The gorilla looked sullen, his colleague talked too easily with strangers. But I kept at it.

"You're involved? A friend of mine as well." That wasn't even a lie. I actually knew someone who worked there for the security services.

That broke the ice and I joined them. We didn't talk that much which was a huge relief for me. What I was able to filter out of the chunks of information that emerged between assessments of the ladies writhing on the catwalk and the *Hertha* players writhing on the playing field, confirmed my assessment: The two implied that they were involved in various semi-legal, and possibly illegal, activities in the construction sector and the black economy - amongst other things. They gave me no real facts, but that was not at issue.

After about an hour I felt I could ask.

“Are you guys quite often here?” I said after switching to white wine (9 Euros). “I'm looking for a buddy of mine, he used to come here quite often.”

“Yes, we're part of the inventory,” said the gorilla, who had courageously outed himself as “Schorsch”, “what's the guy's name?”

“Peter. Peter Brecht.”

“Never heard of him”, said Schorsch, “have you, Matze?”

Matze shook his head, it took a few seconds. With him it seemed to take longer before the penny dropped.

“No. What does he look like, perhaps we know him by sight?”

I had a photo of Peter when he was alive on my phone and showed it to them.

“Oh him,” muttered Schorsch. “Yes, I've seen him a few times. He spoke to Kropf, I think.”

“Really,” I was a little surprised. “They know each other?”

“Looks like it, Sherlock” grinned Schorsch and got up

from the stool, which meant, in his case, he hopped down. “I'll be right back, I must have a leak.”

He retreated to the toilets. I decided to squeeze some more information out of Matze.

“Maybe Kropf knows where Peter hangs out,” I speculated, “it would be really great to see him again.”

“I wouldn't know,” replied Matze, and I detected negative vibrations. My instinct told me not to pursue the issue.

We drank in silence and watched the ladies stripping. A beautiful African woman was doing a grass skirt number, in all seriousness. Frumpy and racist all in one - welcome to East Berlin!

I didn't mean it that way.

Well actually, I did.

Schorsch returned after a small eternity, but maybe it just seemed that way. He looked grumpy.

“I need a fag,” he announced, “I'm going outside. Anyone coming?”

We both said yes. Matze enthusiastically, me uneasily. I didn't have my gun, I wouldn't have been let in the club with it. I've already mentioned risks that can't be eliminated completely.

I got my coat and we went outside.

It was raining and I followed Schorsch into the small side street next to the building. Matze was right behind me. My adrenaline was buzzing, there was work for it. In the KFW factory it had snoozed and now compensated with hyperactivity. In other words, I was in a slight panic. I tried to dismiss it as paranoia - we were just going outside for a smoke.

We stopped under a shelter designed to provide relief to nicotine addicts. I offered my *Ecksteins* to the boys. They were bowled over.

“Holy crap,” laughed Schorsch, “I haven't seen those since school. They're still being sold?”

“I only smoke these,” I said, and lit their cigarettes. We puffed for a while and I told the enthusiastic tobacco connoisseurs where they could order the herb.

I was standing between them and had the impression that they were moving closer to me. Matze now completely blocked the view to Boxhagener Strasse and the rain pattered very loud on the shelter's plastic roof.

Schorsch blew a cloud of smoke in my face. I gasped for breath, my eyes watered. An *Eckstein* has that effect.

“So,” Schorsch said in a chatty tone, “you're looking for Peter Brecht...”

Shit.

“Yes, I... haven't seen him for ages...”

“To be honest, man, we do know him.”

Matze was now stretched up in front of me. He was thin but seemed well trained. It looked like my third beating within 24 hours. A personal record.

“I like you, pal,” Schorsch declared, “please don't take

this personally...”

It was an old-fashioned stomach blow. My abs weren't the toughest, I trained just enough to look good in swimwear. My knees almost buckled. I pulled myself up but Matze immediately grabbed me by the hair and shoved me down, while Schorsch kicked my knee. They weren't doing this kind of thing for the first time.

I calculated the odds, they were miserable. It was different with Fatso and Fausto: They were both stupid and primitive. Here I was dealing with two professional thugs, was unarmed and in a blind alley. So I did the right thing: I dropped to the floor and begged for mercy.

“Please stop,” I blurted out, “Please, I'm sorry, I didn't want...”

Schorsch kicked me in the groin.

“You didn't want what?” he asked quietly, as I writhed and groaned. My behavior seemed to surprise him.

“I didn't know you had a problem with him. I have nothing to do with him!” I sniveled.

“Why are you looking for him?” Matze wanted to know and unceremoniously stubbed out his cigarette on my forehead.

“He owes me money,” a flash of genius, “quite a lot and I'm chasing it! Honestly, that's all! We aren't friends!”

Matze and Schorsch grinned at each other. That was an awkward moment. There were too many unknowns here. What was the relationship between Peter Brecht and these two? They seemed to know but not like him. Did they know he was dead? Had one of them knocked me on the head this morning? Did they know who I was? Or did they know nothing, had nothing to do with it and just did what they would do to anyone who was too nosy?

The two grabbed my arms and pulled me up. I expected more violence and made up my mind to muster all my combat skills even if my chances were poor. But it wasn't necessary - for the time being.

"We're taking you upstairs," said Schorsch. "And don't try any funny stuff."

Matze took a Bowie knife out of his jacket, he apparently kept it within reach, in a sort of holster. I promised to behave. As we climbed the stairs to the top floor, with Matze following behind, I thought of Amanda and those magnificent breasts that had been slapped around my ears just a few hours ago and I wondered whether they had been worth it.

The answer was: Absolutely.

On the top floor of the three-story building, the door opened to a new dimension.

At least that's what it felt like, because whereas the *Blue Flamingo* itself and the rest of the house exuded the battered but cozy atmosphere of the upscale proletariat, this part of the house was a palace. We first passed through a heavy, wrought-iron door that was opened by a prizefighter. If you're wondering where the boxers who don't make it finish up: they are doorkeepers in gangsters' hideaways. They keep unwanted visitors from going through the doors and throw others out of them. That seems to be the only career option apart from selling grilling machines.

Once inside I must admit, I was speechless. What Hartmut Kropf had created here made me envious: The attic and top floor had been combined and six meters above us several large skylights had been installed through which the starry sky was visible - when it wasn't pelting with rain, as it was now. The roof was supported by long columns, not of marble, but they still looked classy. Kropf had built himself a huge loft.

I won't bore you by describing that vast space in great detail; especially since I had the feeling I wouldn't be here very long. Imagine a sort of throne room that a king might have if monarchies had been invented in the 21st Century: Designer furniture, a huge, flat-screen TV showing hardcore porn without audio (there were attractive women and ugly men, so it was probably German), expensive carpets, several large chandeliers and a small gym with high-end fitness equipment in a corner.

A man was toiling away at one of them. Apart from him, me, the boxer-doorman and my two companions no one was in the hall and the boxer soon sneaked out and closed the door.

"Boss," Schorsch called out to the man, "this is the guy."

The boss, in his fifties, I reckoned, in a T-shirt and sweat pants, calmly finished his crunches and groaned as he stood up. He wiped his neck with a towel and walked slowly towards the middle of the hall where we stood. He gazed at me warily but with a smile. I was still somewhat bruised and probably didn't impress him much. And that's how I wanted it. An innocuous ninny who knew nothing, that was my line of defense.

"Have you searched him," the guy asked no one in particular.

Matze replied sheepishly: "No, sorry..."

He frisked me while Schorsch emptied my pockets. He pocketed my cigarettes with a grin, the bastard, but left the money in my wallet. They had their own special style. I worked out the details of my story and hoped I'd get a chance to tell it.

The Boss studied my ID. He wasn't as muscular as could be expected from someone with a private fitness center, had a bald head and large, watery eyes.

"Philip Eckstein," he read and looked at me suspiciously. I wondered if he had heard of me. I was sure I had never met Hartmut Kropf. I had seen his picture in various newspaper articles but I'd never had anything to do with him.

"Funny," grinned Matze, "the same name as his fags?"

"Yeah," chuckled Schorsch and showed Kropf the *Eckstein No. 5*. "Does the company belong to him?"

I said nothing.

Kropf ignored the cigarettes. He had something else on his mind. He came closer and was standing about two feet in front of me.

"Are you a Jew?" He asked.

I had absolutely no idea how to reply. The craziest scenarios raced through my head - would he want to see my circumcised cock to establish if I was Jewish? In addition to everything else, I now had to deal with a raging anti-Semite. This was the end. But you know what?

There was only one possible answer.

"Yes, I am."

Silence. Kropf said nothing, Schorsch and Matze didn't seem to know where their boss stood on religion in general and Judaism in particular. They exchanged uneasy glances. Matze grabbed my arm as a precaution.

Kropf hesitated. Perhaps he had hoped for a different answer. But though I was not even a half-Jew (I'll need to have a closer look to figure that out), I had no choice. I never went into the synagogue, because I believe religion is evil and responsible for a large part of mankind's misery. Berlin's Jewish community knew nothing about me. But if someone in Germany asks you if you are a Jew, you say “Yes”. That's how it is. A rabbi in Friedenau did that the other day when a group of Arab youths had a go at him and they then beat him up badly. The youthful heroes also threatened his young daughter who was with him. Perhaps it was foolish to wear a skullcap in public, but does a rabbi have a choice?

“Brecht owes you money?” Kropf said finally. “That fits. Everyone owes you money, right?”

I kept my mouth shut. It was a very hairy moment and I could do little to control it.

Kropf jerked his head toward a group of black leather seats which represented the throne in the throne room. Matze shoved me into one of the chairs. Kropf sat down opposite me, Matze and Schorsch on the couch. No one bothered to offer me a cup of tea.

“Let's hear your story, Jew”, Kropf growled.

“When I said that Brecht owes me money, that wasn't quite right,” I started with an admission to lend the rest of the story more credibility. “I work for a debt collection agency. Brecht is in arrears with installments for his iPad and car. I always say if you can't afford stuff, you shouldn't buy it, don't you think?”

Kropf didn't answer, he just listened.

“He was never in his apartment,” I continued, “By

chance I ran into one of his friends who wanted to visit him – I don't know his name. He told me that he was often in the *Blue Flamingo*. I thought I'd give it a try."

"You're really stuck into your job," Kropf scoffed. "You even get beaten up ..."

"Tough times. I can reclaim the strip club bill as expenses. But I had no idea that Herr Brecht had so many fans here."

Schorsch showed Kropf the picture of Brecht on my phone. I had totally forgotten that.

"Where'd you get that picture?" Kropf asked.

"I'm a detective," I answered and it was important that it came quickly and without hesitation. "I told you, right? Investigators and Credit Enquiries are linked. We know a lot about people and have photos as well."

"Privacy is just a myth," said Kropf. He stared at me and I had no idea what was going on in his head.

He got up and went in the direction of a desk with a computer. He clicked through a few pages, typed something.

"Philip Eckstein, private investigation," he said aloud, when he found what he had looked for. "You're in the phone book but don't have a website?"

For a gangster he really knew his stuff and I respected him for doing his own research. On the other hand, it was possible that none of his flunkeys could use a computer.

"I may create one, but right now I'm doing okay without," I replied.

"Jews don't need to advertise, right?" said Kropf and came towards me. "You have your own network and things are put your way."

There's no clever answer to that. I didn't want to

provoke Kropf. Mainly because something had caught my eye: standing quietly hidden in a corner of the room stood - a lawn mower.

It's psychologically very effective to show the offender the torture instruments, even the Spanish Inquisition knew that. Maybe it was pure decoration to maintain the owner's reputation.

“I'm just small fry,” I defended myself. “I manage, as I said, nothing more. Debt collection keeps me afloat.”

He stood in front of me and stared again. Suddenly the first blow struck me in the face.

I was so surprised I felt no pain, I was stunned.

“You come and snoop around my club?” Kropf barked. Matze and Schorsch stood up to lend a hand. They grabbed my arms and held me to the armchair while Kropf landed one blow after another on me.

Fortunately, he wasn't as strong as he thought but I yelled blue murder every time he hit me. Most blows were more like smacks. He was well aware that that was more humiliating.

“You asshole!”

Wham!

“Who do you think you are, Jew?”

Bam!

“I'm Hartmut Kropf!”

Zamm!

“I'm the King of Berlin!”

Pamm!

And so on, but after about two minutes he had let off enough steam. I was quite dazed and tasted blood in my mouth. A few times I had blubbered “don't” or “no”. If you have lost respect for me as a tough guy, I would point out that these people had no qualms about killing me. I preferred to take the blows since I had no other choice, there was no need to play the hero.

"Chuck him out," growled Kropf, when he was done, Schorsch and Matze dragged me downstairs and threw me out of the back door into the pouring rain.

"Thanks for the fags", bawled Schorsch, "and no offence, this was your own fault!"

He was right. I pulled myself together and staggered out of the alley towards Boxhagener Strasse, I was displeased with the world. Why the hell was I doing this? For a woman? Seriously? What was wrong with me?

I stopped on the way to visit Emergency at the Urban Clinic. It wasn't busy but they don't ask too many questions - this is Kreuzberg, it happens all the time, even on weekdays. My teeth were still there but the doctor advised me to go to the dentist. My nose was not broken, I had escaped with bruises and a laceration on an eyebrow.

On the way home I had the opportunity of finding someone to blame for the whole fiasco. It was silly, because Hartmut Kropf was mainly to blame. He had beaten me up, nobody else. Nowadays we have a strange tendency to ignore the obvious culprits and to focus on those indirectly involved. If a child is abused by parents, the Youth Welfare Office is to blame. If an offender re-offends, the justice system was too lenient. The airport wasn't ready in time, that means the mayor must somehow be to blame. It depended on how best you could push a story to make it a scandal. People always forget that they are responsible for their own actions. We have almost abolished personal responsibility. Everyone is just a victim of circumstance or unpredictable forces.

Having said that: *My penis* was to blame for everything!

The bastard had persuaded me to get involved with Amanda. If I had kept a cool head, I would have escorted the lady out of my office and made it clear I wanted nothing do with her problems. But a heaving bosom, a rounded ass and I was no longer a professional, just a drooling slave.

Let's not be unfair, maybe it wasn't just my penis. There was something more between us, at least on my side. I want to make clear that I don't fall in love. That calls for strength of character. Love is not automatic, you can control it. Many women say "I want to fall in love again", and they do it, they are in full command of their hormones. Women want to fall in love because they were persuaded at a young age by Walt Disney and the Grimm Brothers that it is the key to a happy life. But even though I'm immune to it (in my opinion) the whole package of this amazing woman, as she still was in my eyes, made me lose my mind short term.

It also seemed clear that Kropf and his cronies had nothing to do with the matter. Anyway, they hadn't recognized me and you're not likely to forget someone you've just knocked on the head that quickly.

I had turned on my phone on the way to the Urban Clinic and now it rang.

"Phil, you asshole!"

That was the endearing voice of Kriminalhauptkommissarin Lisa Becker. She seemed annoyed. Or maybe she was a secret admirer of my perky ass.

“What's up, Lisa?”

“What's up? What's your client up to? She didn't show up and won't answer her phone!”

“I've no idea”, I lied automatically. My penis ordered me to. “My assignment is over and I'm not her dad.”

“Tell me, do you actually check your clients before you take their money, you prick?”

“Usually,” I evaded the issue. I guessed there was trouble ahead.

“Then check this,” said Lisa, “Peter Brecht, our well preserved corpse, doesn't have a sister!”

I almost crashed into a Ford Fiesta.

Fascinating lady

Have you ever hit a woman? Now, this is a question for male readers. Women constantly whack each other, as I learnt from *Dynasty*. I've never hit a woman, at least not against their will, and certainly not in the face. Ahem.

But Amanda was now in for it.

You will be pleased to hear that it gave me no satisfaction and I repented immediately. It is so pathetic, so unmanly. Many men believe violence is the manliest thing in the world but hitting a woman who is physically much weaker is the opposite. In early James Bond films Bond, even Roger Moore, hit women a couple of times. Very feeble. I'm not sure if it's still the case, I rarely watch them. I refuse to see James Bond as a trigger-happy, humorless bodybuilder who, when put into a tuxedo, looks like a bouncer.

However I had taken so much stick today because of Amanda that I thought she should now have her fair share. Gino had closed the shop and wiped the tables when I returned. Amanda had apparently made herself useful as a waitress and caused many a male guest to hang around for an hour or two longer, Gino told me later.

"Phil, at last!" had she greeted me as I stumbled in, "I was really worried..."

A controlled slap in the face, not too hard, but hard enough to make her stumble. I said nothing, but turned to a stunned Gino.

"Give me a double, Gino."

He was about to say something, probably wanting to play the shining hero, but he had known me long enough to be able to read my facial expression. I looked like this only if a client had cheated me of my fee or someone described Daniel Craig as the greatest James Bond. He went to the bar and fixed me a drink.

It is to Amanda's credit that she didn't cry. She clutched her cheek and gave a few quiet groans, but kept quiet otherwise. I regretted it immediately: she deserved it and she knew it. She didn't play the persecuted innocent. Damn, I was suddenly not even angry with her any more.

I sat at the bar with my back to her and enjoyed my Scotch. It was entirely up to her what she did next.

“You've had a rough time.”

She spoke quietly, in the caring, motherly tone that makes a man weak. She was good, really good.

She sat beside me, with her back to the counter. Her eyes slid over my cuts and bruises. My lower lip was swelling gradually.

“I suppose that's my fault?”

She smiled and somehow managed to convey sincere regret. I didn't look at her, but felt her run her fingers over my lips. I winced with pain. She stroked my cheek and then the bandaged eyebrow. Then her hand slipped down the back of my head to my neck. I am happy to announce that even after this near-death experience my arch enemy, aka my penis, still enjoyed excellent health.

She bent towards me.

“I'll be really careful,” she breathed and kissed me infinitely gently on my lips. The pain disappeared instantly. She was an enchantress. Well maybe more of a witch.

Gino joined in.

“Listen, lovebirds. Your strange sadomaso relationship leaves me cold. As far as I'm concerned you can whip each other and push stuff up your butts. But unless you need me as an audience, I suggest you get lost. I need to catch some sleep.”

We went back to my apartment to continue the conversation and fill out the gaps. Then I would throw her out, that was quite clear. To Ninety percent. Or seventy. Well, no less than fifty.

“Say what you have to say”, I said and lit a cigarette. I didn't offer her one. *Ecksteins* are expensive.

I stood at the window, she sat on the sofa and played nervously with her necklace.

“Amanda is my real name. But not Brecht, Luft. Amanda Luft. I can show you my ID card, if you like...”

I considered refusing, but then I took her purse from her handbag and looked at not only her ID but everything else. Documents were issued to Amanda Luft and the identity card was guaranteed real. She was in fact 32, so she hadn't lied about her age.

While I was at it I went through the contents of her handbag. Amanda watched me sullenly but said nothing. She had her own cigarettes in it, *Gauloises*. The usual feminine knickknacks. A pack of condoms. A small, sharp penknife. And a Kindle, standard version.

Fascinating lady, don't you think?

I flicked the knife open. Amanda jumped. It was as if she became aware that she was alone with a man who had suffered violence on her behalf. And who, if necessary, could cause her harm. She was tough, but physically weaker than me.

“Keep talking”, I said and stabbed a spider that was crawling down the wall with the knife. I must hire a cleaning lady again.

“Peter and I met about a year ago”, she continued. “He came straight out of jail. I found him hot, he found me hot. It wasn't love, we were just on the same wavelength. I have a criminal record. Conning people now and then, there were these guys who printed the prettiest 50-euro notes and I helped to distribute them. And some other stuff, but I was never caught.”

“How do you manage all that in addition to your job as a nurse, you saint?”

“I'm not a nurse. I only do casual work and have been looked after by men, who take advantage of me.”

Her tone had changed, now she was bitchy and defiant. I let her run on without showing any emotion.

“I always meet the wrong guys. Maybe there are no right guys, no idea. In the end, I stopped trusting men, they always at some point take you for a ride. Either they sleep with someone else or don't give you your fair share or lie to you in a thousand different ways. Sorry, Phil, but there comes a point when you can't afford to be honest and think only of yourself. You no longer want be the fall guy.”

That sounded... familiar.

“A few weeks ago he came to me, very excited. I didn't live with him, I live in a flat share nearby.”

“Not in Siemensstadt?”

She laughed. “No, but it always sounds very convincing. Does anyone live in Siemensstadt?”

I couldn't think of anybody. I still don't know anyone who does. Very mysterious.

“Someone had spoken to him about a transport job.”

“Smuggling?”

“Something like that. I don't really know what it is all about. Peter spoke about a 'suitcase'. He himself didn't know what was in it but it was worth millions, the contractor apparently mentioned ‘umpteen’ millions. Peter's share was so huge that he would never again have to work.”

“What was he supposed to do?”

“The suitcase will arrive in Berlin in the next few days, probably tomorrow. The sale will take place here. Then the case must be taken to its destination in the United States. That was Peter's job. Don't ask me why the goods couldn't be delivered to America direct, I don't know.”

Too bad, that was my next question. Oh well, lots of other questions remain unanswered.

“What was your role in this?”

“Peter didn't trust the contractor. He wanted to stage a changer with me and needed a second person for that. Got it? I take the real case, he carries the fake to the boss and if he hasn't been conned, he hands over the real one.”

“Clever”, I said, “but risky.”

“As we now know.”

“No, but that's not the reason. Not if the suitcase isn't in Berlin yet. You have never seen it, right?”

“No,” Amanda admitted, “but what does it all mean? Peter has been killed. Do you think it was a coincidence?”

“That's very possible, I have experienced the strangest coincidences. I used to have sex with the sister of a girlfriend. And neither of us realized it.”

“A truly inspiring anecdote, Phil.”

She gradually regained her self-confidence. That did

not suit me at all, but we had to get on.

"Any idea why the contractor would want to kill Peter?"

She groaned. She had a great variety of groans. I knew most of them by now.

"No idea, perhaps they somehow suspected that he would play dirty. Or they no longer wanted him in the deal and had to eliminate him. My God, I hope he didn't mention me!"

She looked at me startled, but I didn't believe she'd had that idea for the first time.

"And you don't know the Berlin client?"

"No. Anyway he's just a middleman. The buyer is in the United States. Absolutely no idea who it is."

"It's probably not important. Do you think that Hartmut Kropf is the middleman?"

She considered feverishly or so it seemed. I had reached my limits when it came to detecting whether she was lying.

"Now you mention his name, I am convinced he is. Peter had most of his contacts at the club and Kropf is a really big cheese."

"He informed me that he is the King of Berlin."

She laughed again, very softly.

"I met him once, in a bar in Friedrichshain, with Peter. Peter had a very healthy respect for him. I found him rather unimpressive, nothing special. I like dangerous men, you know, but he left me cold. I don't know if he's the middleman. Maybe he's in on the deal, that he has a share in it or something."

"What else do you know?"

"Nothing more, I'm afraid. The suitcase will be

delivered by ship."

"By ship?" I gaped.

"Yes, from Poland. Peter mentioned 'mid-week'. This week. In the evening."

It was Tuesday, actually Wednesday.

"Which harbor?"

She shook her head and leaned back on the sofa. The Moon shone through the window and shimmered on her breasts.

I sat down beside her and stared at her. She stared back and tried to interpret my look. But I knew the game. I didn't know how to proceed, so I kept her guessing.

There were several factors to consider. I now knew of an illegal deal which was to take place in Berlin within the next few days. My informant was not very helpful in this respect, but it was my duty to inform the authorities. First thing in the morning I would call Lisa Becker. She could grill Amanda and at the same time offer her a way out. Immunity from prosecution, maybe even a new identity.

That was rather far-fetched. It was more likely they would lock her up while time was running out. I liked Lisa but she was, after all, a civil servant. She was still young and wouldn't mess up her career just to do me a favor.

I was certain that Amanda was lying again. I reflected that I could work her over a bit with her sharp knife. But no, I didn't have the balls. That much self-knowledge I had.

Then there was the umpteen-million-Euro-factor.

You may have noticed, I'm not what you'd call a model citizen. The law is a wonderful thing, but if nobody adheres to it, why should I be the doofus who does?

Especially since it always seems to stand between you and your luck. I would never hurt anyone who didn't deserve it, I'm not a criminal, I have both pride and a code of honor.

But a unique opportunity seemed to be just round the corner. Even if I couldn't use it because I didn't have all the information yet, I could still try to grab at the chance. What could go wrong? The deal could fall through and I would never know it, or it could take place with other protagonists, which came to the same thing. Or I could find a way to wangle myself into the story and snatch a suitcase that contained the stuff that dreams are made of.

“What are you thinking?” asked Amanda getting impatient.

Instead of answering, I stretched out and grasped her right breast, impulsively. Even through her sweater and bra I could feel the nipple harden. She moaned softly. This lady got excited if she sensed danger. That was something that I knew about her.

“What I’m thinking?” I continued caressing her with relish. “I think you haven't told me the whole truth. Of all that stuff, at least half of it is a lie.”

She didn't answer, instead she laid her hand on mine and encouraged me to carry on. She moaned loudly, her eyes closed.

“You used me to figure out who's behind the deal. You didn't give a shit that I was in danger.”

“Yes...” she gasped “you're right! Oh God, keep going...”

“Get undressed.”

The order came before I had consulted my brain.

She smiled wickedly and happily. Gino's humorous

remark earlier on seemed to have a kernel of truth. She enjoyed the situation.

She stood up and pulled her sweater over her head. Then she stepped out of her jeans. She had no pantyhose. She leaned over to me as she undid the bra clasp and freed her breasts. She brushed her cool bare tits over my battered face, but I felt no pain. She smelled of the tobacco smoke in Gino's Bar And a lemon perfume. And sex.

“I'm horny,” she whispered. “Please, Phil… do it…”

I didn't answer, but she could see what was happening in my pants. But there was no triumph in her eyes, no mockery on her lips. Just desperate greed. She dropped on her knees in front of me.

“Do with me what you want,” she moaned, “what you always wanted to do with a woman. It doesn't matter what it is. Use me. I need it now. Please!”

No idea who was in control at that moment. I certainly wasn't, but neither was she. Virtually no one can act that well.

“Turn around,” I ordered.

She did as she was told and stretched her shapely, rounded rump towards me. Her pink slip was wet between her legs, even in the moonlight you could see the spot clearly. She was dripping wet.

I brought out my arch enemy, who got me into this trouble, who was to blame for a whole lot of pain, but also a lot of fun and possibly a lot of money. I gave him another chance, and just two seconds after he was out of my pants, he went all the way down into the hot, wet cave offered to him so freely.

Amanda writhed and jerked her head up. She gave a

spine-tingling cry. She came instantly.

I grabbed at the slip and tore it with a jerk. It was a flimsy thing that now stuck uselessly to her thigh. I pushed into her as far as I could go.

"Hit me, please," she pleaded.

This time I hit her wide ass not her face. My hands whacked her, left and right, her flesh wobbled and quivered. She cried and moaned and moved her pelvis towards me all the time.

"Harder," she demanded, "harder!"

I had lost all control, she had regained it. I was completely in her power, under her spell, I didn't stand a chance. I surrendered to her and she collected the spoils of war. We collapsed. I bit into the back of her neck. Decisions had been made.

Looking for Sean

There you are. What have you been up to since you read the last chapter? I mean, I've been waiting and waiting...

Maybe I shouldn't describe intimate experiences of this kind in such detail but I'm trying to give a vivid impression of my experiences. In other books, far too many pages are filled with descriptions of half-rotten corpses being taken apart by the coroner - and nobody complains.

I was definitely proud of my performance that night. After all, in the 24 hours previously I had been attacked by a bull terrier, got knocked over the head and been beaten up by gangsters. Yet I could still make a woman happy for the second time that day. To be honest: this time I didn't care whether she was satisfied or not, I thought only of myself. Maybe it was better that way.

Of course, I was absolutely knackered. The exertions had drained my strength after all. Amanda even had to help me undress, which she did with a dedication that made me wonder if she had lied twice over and actually was a nurse. She volunteered to wash and re-bandage my wounds and I gratefully accepted. The tenderness and care with which she treated me stood in stark contrast to her rip-off side. But the meaning was clear, I was her soldier and I had to be fit for the pending campaign, if only to die for her and the fatherland.

I sort that out at breakfast in the café around the corner. It was past ten o'clock, I had needed the rest. Shaved and fairly pain-free, I threw myself at a mountain of scrambled eggs while she sat in her clothes from yesterday and sipped her cappuccino.

"Here's what happens now," I announced. "I'll do my best to find out where the suitcase is. I already have a couple of ideas, if they lead nowhere, we're out of luck. If we don't make it in time, it's your fault because you didn't tell me the truth. The whole business should be completed by Friday, you'll stay with me until then and I'll look after you. After that we go our separate ways."

If that's what you want. That's what I wanted to add because I would have preferred that she stay with me. I don't know if you have been in a situation where you wanted someone to vanish from your life and, at the same time, wish the person would stay forever. I watched her as she stirred her coffee and licked the milk foam the spoon. She didn't raise any objections.

"What happens if we actually find the suitcase?" she asked, quite the shrewd businesswoman.

"That depends. We don't know what's inside. Or do we?"

My trained gaze made children cry but she didn't bat an eyelid.

"No, Phil, I wish I did."

"If it's cash, we keep it and split fifty-fifty," I said. "It's probably dirty money for some diabolical enterprise, an American election campaign, for example. It's more complicated if it's valuables. I know how to get rid of jewelry and gemstones. I have contacts for works of art. One has one's network. But you must realize that there are rational limits."

She raised an eyebrow, nothing else moved in her face. It was apparently the first time she heard of "rational limits".

"That means," I continued, "if the amount was correctly described, that is 'umpteen millions', we hand over the suitcase to the authorities. Not out of civic responsibility, but because we could never get rid of it on the market without taking irresponsibly high risks for our freedom and health. Something that valuable is not guarded by a single security officer, but half an army, and I don't have an army."

Amanda smiled, slightly. "You are an army for me."

"Three guys knocked me about yesterday. And to be honest, two would have managed as well."

"You forgot your gun."

"You can't rely too much on that," I growled and scraped the remains of the scrambled eggs off my plate. "It's just a small caliber pistol, for defense."

"It would have been enough for those crooks."

"I'm a good shot." I wasn't bragging, I really am. "But aside from the highly-charged nature of the situation, I wouldn't *want* to kill anybody. I defend myself with a gun, if need be. I could have shot the pooch's owner, I would've had the right, but I didn't. What I'm saying is: my risk tolerance has limits, both in terms of the risk situation and the magnitude of the booty. This applies even when I'm no longer your knight in shining armor."

I could see she was disappointed. She needed me, but my rules didn't apply for her. That meant, never turn your back to her, Phil. Ideally, she would turn her back to me. But preferably her chest. I realized more and more that what motivated me was not so much dosh but the hope for more Amanda in future.

"Out of interest," I murmured, "what kind of panties are you wearing, I ruined yours?"

Her smile was so hot, my hair ached.

"None. Feels really great."

I hadn't mentioned one option as regards the suitcase. We didn't know what kind of case it was, it might well contain nuclear material. You might find this a bit nutty, and yes, I've definitely seen too many James Bond movies (those starring Daniel Craig). But in the USA there are more unbalanced multi-millionaires than anywhere else in the world (in Hollywood alone an estimated ten thousand), and one of them might think: I could blow the White House into orbit and then proclaim a new dictatorship where the rich upper class treats the rest of the population as slaves without rights. Most Americans wouldn't even notice the difference.

I wouldn't open a suitcase that looked suspicious. But what does a suspicious suitcase look like? I was clearly operating beyond my capacity. On the other hand: If the suitcase could be entrusted to a nobody like Peter Brecht, then I was well qualified. Bottom line, I thought it most likely that the goods came from the art history sector. Perhaps relics. A local expert was needed to check the authenticity; that would explain the detour via Berlin. I went with the flow, I was fishing in murky waters and my chances of success were minimal anyway.

I didn't regard Hartmut Kropf as a lead. There was no real reason link him to the story. He knew Peter but so did a lot of small, medium and big criminals in Berlin. He didn't seem to know he was dead, at least nothing of the kind was mentioned, nor did he ask about him. That left room for speculation, of course, but of one thing I was sure: None of those three merry fellows had ever seen me before, unlike the killer, to whom I owed my scabby head wound and other cuts which I blocked out with an effective combination of paracetamol and coffee. I had guzzled two pots in the café and on our way to the city center I had some in a paper cup which Amanda fed me. Being cared for by her was indescribably good. I wanted more.

The fact was, we had just one real clue.

Somewhere beyond the sea
Somewhere waiting for me
My lover stands on golden sands
And watches the ships that bring a suitcase

I shouldn't really know this song at my age.

As with most people from the Ruhr, a substantial amount of Polish blood pulsed through my veins. After Germany's first attempt at a World War, a lot of hard-working hands were required and were imported from Poland. Integration went smoothly which is why the most famous resident from there is popular TV detective *Schimanski*. No one noticed that, or that he was played by a Berliner. There are of course countless "owskis". They are also typical Berliner names. The place is full of owskis: Grabowski, Lewandowski, Buschkowsky, Quassowski, Tschüssikofski. These names refer to the place of origin or family background. Herr Buschkowsky comes from the bush, Herr Grabowski from the grave. It's good when a thriller contributes to your general knowledge, right?

Not really? Okay, I'll carry on.

Hackescher Markt is a well-known tourist trap in Berlin. I'm sure you know it, so I will only briefly mention that outdoor catering again committed an ecological capital crime, i.e. it was using patio heaters even though the weather was perfectly okay. It hadn't rained and it was a cozy 17 centigrade, which I found pleasant, but was apparently too chilly for Russian tourists who must be spared arctic temperatures. I'm not an eco-freak, but I've switched to a provider offering renewable energy, not because of what happened in Japan, but because I believe it's important! I switched a month before it happened, I've got it in writing! My main motivation was not having a guilty conscience about leaving appliances in stand-by, or keeping the fridge too cold, leaving the hall light on and so forth. The best way to rid yourself of this terror is to get green electricity. The issue is solved and you can be as wasteful as you like. *That's* what their advertising should be about, not the eternal "We have only borrowed the earth from our children." That sounds like a tax dodge.

I made a bee-line for the Irish pub on the other side of the railway station. In high season it was packed with British travelers who felt an insatiable thirst for Guinness or ravenously hungry for stew (which is delicious here, by the way), it was half empty this morning. Breakfast was over, and there were only a few lonely coffee and beer drinkers.

I was very fond of this pub, the atmosphere was not really authentic, it served up system gastronomy, but a German wouldn't notice that anyway. Everything was decorated in green and wood, I liked it that way. That's how I would furnish my apartment, but I didn't want lady visitors to think I was a color blind serial killer.

"I'm looking for Sean," I informed the cute waitress in English, after ordering my Guinness, always the globetrotter.

"Ick gloob, der kommt gleich rinjeschneit," she answered and stalked off.

I was picking the blood off my head (I'm not easily embarrassed, but that was a really low blow), when the waitress' words came true: Sean O'Briain took the stage. The spelling is important. It's pronounced "O-Breean", and Sean does not like being called "O-Brian". Don't dare.

Sean chatted a bit with the bartender. The two were friends, even though you got the impression the bartender was afraid of the broad-shouldered, 50 year old Irishman. It was inevitable because Sean had acquired a manner that intimidated everyone: piercing eyes, a cynical grin (like mine), a body posture that testified: "I can make plum jam of you and feed it to your mother." He was slightly taller than me, muscular, even though I couldn't imagine him in a gym. He had his red hair cut twice a year, he had told me, otherwise he just let it grow wild. He wore tweed and leather and always the same gear. His appearance didn't matter to him at all and I respect that. Luckily personal hygiene did.

"Hi, Sean," I called to him and he waved back contentedly. I had indicated that I wanted a chat, so he shuffled over to my table.

"Morning, Phil," he greeted me with a firm handshake. "Haven't seen you for a while. Thought you were dead."

"No, I'm not."

"Fancy that."

Sean's Guinness arrived before mine, I wasn't

surprised, but he waited until I had mine and we were able to clink glasses.

We always started with football, it was mandatory. I had checked the latest developments in the Premier and Irish Leagues on the Internet especially for him. I didn't give a shit any more after I discovered there was not a single football player I liked. I felt sorry for football fans because they get psyched out about trivialities. I loath FIFA and every single football reporter from the bottom of my soul. I wanted nothing to do with it. Apart from that, VfL Bochum had just been relegated for the sixth time, and enough is really enough. Life's too short and crappy anyway.

"I could use your help, by the way," I finally came to the point, as if I had just come up with it.

"It's an honor," he growled. Sean owed me a favor, he knew that. He had thumped a rebellious colleague too hard. That had ended in a long hospital stay and with the threat of imprisonment. My eyewitness account of the affair stated clearly that Sean had acted in self-defense and the other guy had started it. That was not strictly true, but my conscience was clear. The other guy was a pimp of the worst variety, he threw his girls out of open windows if he was displeased with them. Besides, it was always good to keep on the good side of people like Sean.

He was in the retail business, by which I mean that he was one of Berlin's most important fences. He could even supply weapons, if only on a small scale. When I had shown him my Walther P22 he nearly fell off the stool laughing, he called it a "girl's gun" and offered me an unregistered PPQ with 15 shots. Cheek, after all, the P22 is the best selling small-caliber gun in the world! I was really offended, drank too much and shot the 'Emily' mascot off his Rolls Royce. I thought my time had come, but Sean congratulated me and said that poofy English symbol had always annoyed him. He never replaced it.

"If you expected a delivery from Poland by water," I speculated, "where would the ship dock?"

"What kind of delivery," Sean asked. "Something big?"

"No, small. Portable."

"My Polish deliveries come via the Havel," he explained. "The Spree is better policed for some reason, the customs blokes believe it's enough to police one river."

"The Havel? Spandauer Hafen?"

"That's it."

That was useful. Spandau harbor was relatively small. We now had the place and the approximate time. Maybe more?

"Say, can you name a couple of ships which sometimes deliver stuff out of turn," I asked as diplomatically as possible.

Sean looked at me a warily, as if he was afraid I might be bugged.

"Are you looking for something specific?"

"Yes."

"Not the usual?" He didn't say any more than that. As far as I was concerned, he could trade with Azerbaijani unicorns.

"The captain would have to be very experienced and trustworthy."

"Not many of those around," Sean grinned and drank a second Guinness, which was placed unasked under his nose. "There's Pawel."

"Pawel," I inquired.

"Yes. Pawel Nowak. His boat's called *Zuzanna.*"

It was awful, he had to spell it. How Sean and his lousy language skills could hold such a position in the Berlin underworld, was a mystery to me. But you could say that about all the clans that had Neukölln and Wedding under control. I still didn't know what had brought him to Germany. Someone made sinister hints about the IRA but I didn't want to snoop.

Perhaps you're wondering why I didn't ask him directly if he had anything to do with it. As a powerbroker in wholesale he was certainly a candidate? Yes, but not as a human being.

He was an adventurer, he delighted in tradition. I've already mentioned his clothes, haven't I? He wasn't rich, his Rolls Royce was a good flagship, but the only luxury in his life. He liked a clear-cut existence without drama and he did only what he had always done. Killing people didn't come into it. We all have our rules of conduct. For him it was not the penal code, but a hodgepodge of Catholic guilt and the straight-thinking of the working class. You don't kill people. For him that was obvious, like opening a door for old ladies or taking a shower after sex.

We talked briefly about the financial crisis and how the attitude of the Irish people to Germany had changed to a mixture of respect and fear. Sean felt that it served his country right. He hadn't been pleased that Ireland had tried to cash in on financial transactions and high-tech to get rich. How did they differ from the British, they were now behaving just like them?

I said goodbye and left. To my great joy (and mild surprise) Amanda was waiting outside, still in my Astra. I didn't want her with me because Sean wouldn't have spared me a single minute if she had been sitting at the table.

"The trail leads west," I said theatrically, as I got behind the wheel.

"You are my shining hero," she whooped and kissed me excitedly.

I pulled the car into Unter den Linden.

Spandau Ballet

I have very rarely been in Spandau, something I had in common with most Berliners who might stray there for the Christmas market or the *Citadel Music Festival.* Many believe Spandau is full of stuffy, bourgeois squares, but it actually has more in common with Neukölln than with Zehlendorf. The charming old Altstadt with the recently prettified waterfront concealed the fact that, away from the center, things get really tough: Some time ago, the police made a list of Berlin's nine "problem neighborhoods", and four of them were in Spandau. The industrial bloodletting had left its mark and Spandau itself had ignored the problem for a long time. On the plus side, however, rents here are among the cheapest in the city, and the houses aren't socialist pre-fabs either. The pleasure-seeking students that invade Berlin want to be near the various party scenes – which means rents in Kreuzberg explode. These students are the guilty party: They push up rent prices but then blame it on ominous "yuppies" who are actually very scarce in that area.

We drove down the road south of the Altstadt center until we were on a level with the port. I parked in a side street, and as Amanda climbed out and looked around, I set up my monitoring equipment. My coat had a special pocket not only for my gun, but also for my binoculars. I loved them: they were compact and light, with ten-fold magnification and image stabilization – a click of a button captured the image so you could quietly examine the image, even though it had changed in real time.

Other essentials: water bottle and chocolate bars. I handed them to Amanda, along with the camera - a proper camera with optical zoom, not cell phone trash. I wasn't expecting to use it because I wasn't investigating, but you never know, and Amanda had a handbag anyway. I left the night vision device in the car boot, it seemed a bit excessive to take it. The port would be illuminated; vessels docked at night as well. Something in me was also reluctant to pull out all the stops for this campaign. Perhaps I didn't really want to find the famous case because I was pretty sure I would then never see Amanda again. She would grab her share and zoom off to Trinidad and / or Tobago. I was chained to Berlin, I couldn't live anywhere else.

We reached the waterside after a few minutes. It is officially known as the Spandau "South Harbor" which is geographical nonsense. There's a ship gas station with the Shell emblem on it where river freighters take anchor in two, sometimes three, rows.

Most of the ships looked similar: flat enough to fit under bridges, about 40 meters long, the majority of them freighters. Some carried ore, others scrap metal. They had an elevated bridge and cabins at the bow and stern. I remember wanting to own a small yacht, but that was now purely academical. Nevertheless, I found this lifestyle very romantic - even if you were just transporting tons of rubble and rubbish.

"Nice here," said Amanda, viewing the surroundings which were not spectacular, but the River Havel and open sky were a nice change from the stone canyons downtown. Ships stretched to the horizon and the harbor was much larger than what was visible to us. But that was incidental, because one thing was certain: if the *Zuzanna* was to grace Berlin with her presence she'd have to pass through here.

We took a walk. Well, we pretended to, we were aware that we were probably not the only ones waiting for the ship. We had to stay on the riverside to watch the ships, there was nowhere to hide. The least we could do was not to attract undue attention. If someone recognized us – tough luck.

"Over there," Amanda whispered excitedly, "a polish Flag!"

She was right; a freighter proudly flew the white and red flag. But it was not the *Zuzanna*, and shortly after we ran into a barrier that marked the end of the public area. We discovered four more Polish ships. Sean was right, Poles enjoyed coming here.

"There's no point traipsing through the entire harbor," I said. "We'd also have to cross to the other side and in the end it doesn't matter. I've checked the map, all the Polish ships come in from the north, through the Altstadt. We just have to wait."

She agreed, so we made ourselves comfortable on a bench. It was still broad daylight and time wouldn't fly, but it was a nice change just to relax and not be bothered by psychopaths.

We watched the ships come and go, the excursion boats that carried white-haired beings to Brandenburg and the small and large motor yachts. My ambitions as regards the latter suffered a setback: The people on these boats all had one thing in common - they were shit ugly. The only other place you find such unattractive people were in the audience of folk music programs, and these people aroused the impression that that's where they were headed. Up to now I had envisaged young, dynamic types in Tommy Hilfiger clothes, I was faced with bloated 50-year olds in leisure wear.

"I can forget that dream," I grinned and told Amanda what I had observed. She thought it really funny.

"You're always good for a surprise," she chuckled.

"Look who's talking" I replied, a little too forcefully. I tried to get her to tell me more about herself but what good would do? I couldn't trust her and she didn't trust me. So we talked politics (she turned out to be surprisingly conservative when it came to dealing with anarchists and squatters), movies (she also disliked Daniel Craig, my dream woman), religion (there's no God - thank God) and Sex. We focused on the latter, we were both trying to lower our guards and maybe put theory into practice. I showed her my P22 and I could see the thing electrified her. Weapons really are a penis substitute in a way. Luckily, I have both.

"Hang on!" she said, in the middle of the conversation and pointed her chin in the direction of a man who strode slowly towards the Altstadt in our direction. "That guy!"

He was in no hurry. I could see his face, but he didn't seem familiar. As he approached, I reckoned he was in his early 30s. Quite a character, with a shaved head, leather jacket and at least twelve tattoos, they weren't visible but just had to be there, otherwise the rest of his appearance made no sense.

"Do you recognize him?" I asked, and we both tried not to stare at him too obviously.

"No," Amanda said, "I thought I did, but I was wrong."

We let him by. He slipped past us, his sneakers made no sound on the concrete strip that served as a walkway. Suddenly he stopped, turned back and looked me in the eye.

"Got a light, man?"

The question was innocent enough. I nodded and he pulled out a pack of *Camels*. I lit one for him and he strolled on unhurriedly. Amanda watched him.

"Nice ass on him," she remarked.

"Yes, delightful," I said.

"Yours is nice too."

"I know."

The guy moved out of sight. After that absolutely nothing happened, until it got dark. Luckily it didn't rain. We stretched our legs now and then and each time we had to find a new bench because the pedestrians pounced at every empty one. It was getting late and soon we were the only ones around, apart from one or two dogs with their proud shit collectors.

"How much longer?" I asked Amanda, who had become silent and morose. Perhaps she thought that another detective would have found out more and she would already be safely on an airplane and the case under her butt.

"Till dawn," she said resolutely.

"Oh, great," I said, "but keep in mind - two hundred a day."

She laughed just a bit too gloatingly and blew me a kiss. "Can I pay in kind?"

Till dawn, eh.

I had bought some croissants, grain rolls and water at a bakery in Klosterstraße earlier on. I have handled observations that took several days and without such pleasant company.

It turned dark. The streetlights lit up, the waterside houses turned their lights on. People were listening to music or watching TV at the close of the day. Amanda snuggled up to me, it was chilly. I assessed my chances of laying her right here when everything was quiet and that kept me going. I had given up the idea that we would achieve anything here. Amanda too, but she had nothing in her life to look forward to.

Except me.

We were silent for a long time, we just kept each other warm. I could feel her soft curves and her breath. She clung to me, and we kissed now and then. We looked like lovers. The perfect disguise, don't you think?

I noticed the *Zuzanna* when she was nearly past us.

It was almost exactly midnight, and you could see a large, dark boat gliding through the water in the dim light, I almost dozed through it. I looked up, the Polish flag on the bow could be seen clearly even in the dark. And then I saw the name.

“Wake up,” I shook Amanda. She blinked and looked around.

“My God,” she whispered, “that's incredible. You were right! Pigs can fly! You were actually right! I thought you got me here to lay me!”

“What made you think that,” I grinned smugly. “Let's see where the good *Zuzanna* is headed.”

Fortunately for us, not too far. The ship docked right next to another similarly sized freighter. Apparently it was quite normal to share a berth, at least if you wanted to save money and weren't too particular about rules and regulations.

I could see two men but just as silhouettes. One was

sitting at the wheel in the cabin, the other jumped on board the other ship with a rope and moored the *Zuzanna.* He shouted something to the mate or captain (a title that seemed a bit over the top for a river truck driver) and jumped back on board. After a while the guy turned off the cabin light and went to the front cabin, where the other one seemed to be because the only light shone through the small window. We could hear music, but didn't recognize what it was, probably Polish.

"Now what?" Amanda asked, her voice vibrating with tension.

What indeed? No idea. I hadn't really believed this situation would actually come about. There was a suitcase with extremely valuable contents on board this barge. Or maybe not. Wasn't it all just speculation? I would have preferred it if the two sailors had taken off, then Amanda and I could have rummaged around but I'd have had to get the flashlight out of the car to do that.

"Let's wait a bit," I suggested.

"Wait, what for? You've got a gun, that counts for something!"

The other Amanda was back. I had almost forgotten her.

"When they're asleep," I explained to her (and me), "it'll be easier. They probably use separate cabins, one in the front and in the back. Then we'd have to deal with only one at a time."

Not bad for a plan that I had just pulled out of the hat. Amanda agreed. We got up and moved further away, because our bench was under a street lamp.

My binoculars did the job. I had a good view into the window of the front cabin. Two young-ish men, it seemed to me, sat drinking and playing cards. They didn't laugh much, they had probably had a long day.

After less than an hour one of them got up and walked along the railing to the rear cabin. A few minutes later his light went out, the guy had gone to sleep.

"Give him a few minutes," I said, "Then we'll try the front cabin, it's bigger and I assume it's the captain lieutenant's den."

"Okay, okay," agreed Amanda, without much enthusiasm. Things were taking too long. Her greed was unlovely, outside the bedroom.

The captain's light was still on, he probably had something to do. I had an idea what it was. What all men do when we haven't seen a woman for a long time, or even just for twelve hours. Anyway, I thought it appropriate to wait until he turned off the light and felt safe.

After a quarter of an hour the time arrived. Amanda had fetched my flashlight and relieved herself in the bushes, she was so nervous. I had my bladder under control, but that's training. Even if I really panic, my senses and organs remain functional. Remember the bull terrier?

"Okay," I said, "let's roll..."

And then stopped. Amanda heard them too.

Voices.

Not from the boats, from somewhere nearby. Mens' voices. Coming nearer.

"Fuck," I exclaimed quietly. "Don't move."

Luckily we were still hidden from sight and moved further back behind a parked van. And then we saw them: Two men, one very tall and gaunt, the other short and robust. I recognized them immediately, because moon happened to come out from behind the clouds.

Matze und Schorsch. My dear friends from the *Blue Flamingo.*

Getting ugly

"I don't believe this," I snarled, "it's them after all!"

Amanda wavered between confusion and uncontrollable rage.

"Phil, who the hell are they?"

"I told you about my adventures in Friedrichshain," I whispered. "Those two gentlemen were my opponents."

Amanda frowned like someone who hadn't been to high school and had firm opinions on pseudo-educated speech wankers, but understood what I meant. She tried not to go ballistic.

"If we hadn't waited," she hissed, "we would have had the suitcase!"

"Or they might've surprise us, caused a stir on the ship, and bumped us off," I suggested, the more likely possibility.

We watched as the two men made their way to the *Zuzanna* and climbed onto the ship in front, the tall Matze much more agile than his round counterpart.

"Surprise is on our side," Amanda whispered excitedly, and rubbed against my back. Heavens, even through three layers of fabric I could feel her sapphire-hard nipples. The woman wasn't normal, a cold, calculating, manipulative... well, woman.

"What do you suggest?" I asked, quite sincerely, because the situation was new to me and I'm not particularly spontaneous.

"Shoot them," she cooed, "they're just two shitty gangsters."

Schorsch and Matze were swinging over the far side to board the *Zuzanna*. They had no idea that a hot blonde had just decided they should die. But I had to make something clear.

"Let me make this clear," I whispered, and firmly grabbed her neck. I have a special grip: thumb on the throat, middle finger in the ear – and you have peace and quiet. "I'm not a murderer. I would kill someone if he threatened my life or that of an innocent. That's all my gun is for. Get the picture?"

"Okay," she gasped, her wistful gaze went right through my heart. I let go on the spot. How did she do it?

"We'll get our chance when they come out," I thought out loud.

"When they've got the suitcase?"

"Yes. Maybe. I said maybe."

It depended on whether the two were armed. A question that would be answered amazingly quickly.

We watched the two men split up: Schorsch the fireball went to the captain's cabin, Matze to the other. No light had come on, so the sailors hadn't noticed anything.

That changed suddenly, because at a sign from Schorsch's hand, they simultaneously opened the small cabin doors and squeezed inside. The lights came on, voices were heard, scuffles - hard to tell from which cabin. There was silence on Matze's side very quickly. Schorsch and the captain, however, had a greater difference of opinion, which ended after a couple of minutes.

With a shot.

It was the familiar very short, dull, *click-bang*! Schorsch hadn't used a silencer. Perhaps he hadn't intended to shoot, or he did not care, but it has to be said that no one who heard the shot called the police. They didn't want to seem idiots, just because a tire had burst or some tosser let off a firework - in Berlin these were always the real reasons. I have these wonderful neighbors who let off their loudest fireworks in the middle of the night with the sole purpose of robbing people of their sleep.

"Shit!" Amanda stared at me with her mouth open. Suddenly she realized this wasn't a game and that our opponents were a size larger than she expected.

I said nothing and just held her. I was afraid she might panic and blow our cover. This much was certain: in a confrontation with the two, I would lose.

We watched Matze come out of the second cabin and turn out the light. He went over to Schorsch as he came out. He turned off the light and closed the door. They discussed something and Matze sounded excited. Schorsch calmed him down and they clambered over the other freighter and then on shore.

Amanda saw it immediately.

"No," she whimpered, "no, no, no..."

She hadn't cried when she heard about Peter Brecht's death, but now tears ran down her cheeks.

Schorsch carried the suitcase.

They had managed it.

And we were left looking on.

"I'm sorry," I whispered, but I was busy trying to keep Amanda quiet, holding her with both arms and covering her mouth. She trembled with anger and disappointment. She had missed the chance of a lifetime because of an idiot like me. There would be no tender loving care for dear Philip, that was for sure.

But she still kept a cool head. Her body relaxed and she calmed down. We watched as the two men strode unhurriedly towards Klosterstraße.

In case you ask, the idea of shooting them in the back came to me. It would have worked. The case would have been ours. I could see that Amanda was playing with the idea too but she didn't dare to express it. I must confess to my shame that my hand had slipped involuntarily to my gun pocket.

But who was I? Gollum?

I don't have a wicked other me that urges me to bump people off so I can get to "my precious". I didn't even know what the "precious" was. And besides - Hartmut Kropf knew me by name! I had to admire the brilliant performance the three gave last night, pretending they had never seen me before. They were in the picture the moment they spotted me at the *Blue Flamingo* bar. I was lucky to be alive and I didn't want to change my luck.

When they finally disappeared, Amanda exploded.

"Fuuuuck!" she wailed and pummeled on my chest with her fists. "It's your fault! You asshole! Son of a bitch! I could be rich! You and your waiting! The suitcase was there all the time and you were playing the Super-Detective! You wanker! You bastard..."

She carried on for a while. I could have pointed out that we were lucky not to have walked into the arms of the two killers, or that without me we wouldn't be here, but I let her scream and curse until she was exhausted. She gave up when she realized that I wasn't impressed by her theatricals.

"Cigarette?" I suggested, and we shared an *Eckstein*. We puffed on it for a few minutes. I needed a little time to sort my thoughts. Lately, one extreme situation had led to another and that is not normal, even for a private investigator.

"We ought to check on the sailors," I said finally, "maybe we can still help them."

Amanda looked at me as if I had accidentally trampled her cat to death.

"What's it got to do with us?"

"They're human beings," I explained. "I understand your disappointment, but there are more important things."

I turned away, thoroughly disgusted by this woman. The last half hour had been an eye-opener, but Amanda would not have been Amanda if she hadn't surprised me once again.

"Wait," I heard her say as I jumped onto the first boat. "I'm coming too."

I took her hand and pulled her up. We kissed briefly, then went silently to the *Zuzanna*. I checked the captain first. What was his name? Correct - Pawel Nowak. May he rest in peace.

I opened the door and switched on the light, which was right next to the door. I had gloves on because quite soon fingerprints would be taken meticulously, and I really had no way to explain all this to Lisa Becker. Ideally, I wouldn't have to.

We didn't see him immediately because the cabin was roomier than expected. It was a cozy little living room, complete with a TV. The sofa had been unfolded to serve as a bed, but Nowak wasn't on it. He had tried to shield himself behind the upholstered chair, but it had been futile.

He lay behind it, trapped and dead with blood still seeping out of the bullet hole in his forehead. I thought about Fausto, who two days ago - it seemed to me like an eternity – had given up his life in the same way.

The body was naked, Nowak had had no time to cover himself. An undignified death, but involuntary death is always undignified. You should take precautions.

“He's dead,” I said, and I must say to her vindication that Amanda very convincingly bit on her lower lip and put her hand on her mouth. Maybe I was too cynical in denying her any human emotions.

“Are you going to call the police,” she asked. She stood in the doorway because she had no gloves on and wasn't stupid.

“Yeah, later,” I said, “but probably anonymously.”

I wasn't keen to shop Hartmut Kropf. I couldn't prove anything and, as I said - the man knew me.

I went back to the door. I noticed Nowak's wallet on the small table against the wall. Out of curiosity I looked through it. Detectives do these things, and they shadow beautiful women on the street just to stay in practice.

“If it's money you're after, I want half” scoffed Amanda, although she might have been serious.

I found the usual stuff in it, money and plastic money, which I didn't touch. The only unusual thing was an electronically stamped ticket.

“He was apparently in the Citadel,” I mumbled.

“Lovely, then he did something interesting in his last hours,” Amanda said smugly, “apart from being shot, which was perhaps more interesting for him.”

“He was there today,” I said, and showed her the ticket.

"So?"

"It's strange because he only got here this evening."

"What are you getting at?"

I didn't know. But there was this tingling sensation that I had known since being a boy watching people post their letters in a fake mailbox.

"Let's check the other guy," I suggested. I pocketed the ticket and we followed the railing to the stern of the freighter.

"We won't be much help to him," Amanda protested, but followed me dutifully.

I opened the door to the smaller cabin and fumbled for the light switch.

Something hit my hand. Something very hard.

"Shit," I yelled and backed away. This time I grabbed my P22 instantly, Amanda screamed and toppled over – she almost fell overboard, but she managed to steady herself.

"Don't move!" I gasped. Fortunately, my left hand had been hit, it hurt like hell, but my right arm was outstretched and the barrel of the gun pointed straight at the open door where I could see a silhouette. Unbelievable, the other guy was still alive!

"Put the light on!"

He did.

We stared at each other. He in panic and me full of amazement. The surprises kept coming, and it had been such a nice, quiet day.

The man was younger than I had expected, no more than twenty-three. He was blond, wiry and pantherlike. Certainly a tough opponent in an encounter. However, I had a loaded and cocked handgun, he had a heavy glass ashtray and my delicate fingers on his conscience.

"Drop it," I ordered and he threw down the ashtray.

"Who are you?" He asked, not me. I found that strange. On the other hand, hey, it was his home, so he was entitled to ask.

"We don't belong to them," was my answer. *No, we are these other people who want to rob you* as well - I should have added. "I won't hurt you."

He didn't believe me, which probably had to do with the gun that was pointed at him. I lowered the gun and he relaxed a little.

Then he saw Amanda and the sight of her seemed to confuse him further. She has that effect on men, but this time perhaps for other reasons. Her presence calmed him down, as if it were impossible to be bumped off by an attractive couple - unless you had advertised in *Happy Weekend*.

"What about Pawel?" I could now hear his Polish accent. My maternal grandfather had probably spoken that way. I never met him though.

"Dead," I replied tersely. "They did it, not us."

He sobbed. Seriously, he didn't curse or struggle for composure, he sobbed and cried like a girl. I don't want to put him down, but I found this reaction quite strange. He staggered into the cabin and sat on the unfolded sofa bed. He wailed and sobbed and said things in Polish.

Amanda and I exchanged glances. It seemed that more than a purely business relationship had came to an end. Well, sure, the two had had their fun for a while. I liked that, at least they had lived their lives as they wanted to. Nowak himself had been, at the most, in his late thirties, much too young to die, but he hadn't been unhappy.

We climbed into the small cabin. Amanda sat next to Pawel and stroked his short blonde hair. Since he was wearing only his underwear, I found this slightly inappropriate, but I said nothing and sat on the doorstep, between the deck and bottom bunk. I put the gun away.

Amanda's fingers worked miracles even with Pawel - no one is *that* gay. The risky situation sounded a chord in her and she surveyed the boy's toned body with pleasure. She needed a good therapist, I thought. But we all have our fetishes. Just because mine - breasts - is generally accepted, doesn't allow me to pass judgment on sexual preferences.

"My condolences," I said after a while. "What's your name?"

"Jan," he whispered, he didn't want to disclose his last name.

"This is Amanda," I introduced the lady, "some call me Phil."

He sniffled and rubbed his eyes. There was a bottle of water, I handed it to him. He drank a little and passed the bottle to Amanda, who was also thirsty. For myself, I had a few questions and we couldn't sit here all night. I should have informed the police long ago. But that was actually Jan's task, I thought.

"How come they didn't hurt you?" I asked.

He jerked his head toward the ceiling. There was, and you could only see it when you looked really closely, a sliding door without a handle. It wasn't completely closed and Jan got up and opened it with a sheepish smile on his face. There was an empty space, big enough for a guy like him.

"You hid there when you heard them coming?" I

asked.

“Yes,” he said. “They wanted to come tomorrow. We're early.”

“They probably anticipated that,” I sighed sympathetically. “Tell us the whole story.”

As we assumed, the suitcase was given to them in Poland with instructions to take it to Berlin. Thursday evening had been the planned delivery time, i.e. in 24 hours time. Why Schorsch and Matze had arrived early, Jan didn't know. Maybe it was just on the off chance.

They probably hadn't intended to eliminate the two carriers. Jan had asked Nowak about it several times, but Nowak had always said that he trusted these people; also, the wages weren't so huge that they would be killed to economize. Maybe they hadn't wanted to kill Nowak. The debate we had heard from the captain's cabin could allow that conclusion. For the moment, it wasn't important.

“When did you arrive in Spandau?” I asked point blank.

He stopped short, then looked at me in astonishment.

“Today,” he said hesitatingly.

“But what time?”

He didn't answer. I wasn't in the mood for games so I showed him the Citadel ticket.

“We just wanted to see the Citadel,” he claimed, without looking at me. “We have passed it so many times, and the weather was great...”

One of the worst liars I have ever met. Amanda almost grinned. And Jan withstood the awkward silence for less than thirty seconds.

“I don't care,” he whispered, “it doesn't matter any more.” And then some sad words in Polish.

He came out with it. They had arrived in the morning. They had moored just behind the Spandau Lock, which separates Havelland from Upper Havelland. The Citadel was just over the bridge.

"We had the suitcase with us."

Those were his exact words, I will never forget them.

Amanda was about to freak out. She had blocked the suitcase out of her mind – as one does to protect the soul. Now lightning flashed through her body, and she was breathing hard with excitement.

"The case with the goods," I asked, also pretty agitated.

"What was in it?" Amanda wanted to know.

"Was tightly closed," said Jan. "Metal box, hammer hard. With the right tools - we could have opened it. But we did not want to take the risk."

"What did you do with the suitcase?"

"Hidden." Jan shrugged his shoulders. He wasn't really bothered. "And second suitcase organized in Szczecin. They have it now, yes?"

I summoned up all my patience and Amanda massaged her own neck so she didn't go berserk. It took a moment to realize he meant Stettin.

Ultimately there was only one question I wanted answered.

"Where exactly is the suitcase?"

Treasure hunt

Have you ever broken into a castle? Neither have I.

Like most Berliners I have never been inside the Citadel. It's one of those things you should do when you have guests but then in the end you take them to Potsdamer Platz and Museum Island. I have never seen the Pergamon Museum or Charlottenburg Palace from the inside. But I know almost every bar, nightclub and currywurst stall. That counts for something.

Amanda wanted to march to the Citadel immediately, it took just 15 minutes. She would have swum through the moat, climbed the wall and knocked down the guards to get at the Nibelungen treasure, but she was tired and so was I.

We said goodbye to poor, unhappy Jan and instructed him to call the police and report Nowak's death, without mentioning details which might incriminate him, and then make his getaway. The *Blue Flamingo* team would notice the fraud soon and come back. Jan understood what was necessary and we parted in friendship.

“Can we go to your place?” Amanda asked. I liked the question but decided against it.

“When our pals realize what's going on, they might come looking for me,” I speculated, as we walked towards my car. “My address isn't a state secret. I don't want to be there right now.”

“Where then?”

“We'll find a hotel.”

We checked into a double room in a small hotel in the Altstadt. It was a beautiful half-timbered house painted white with black wood. I suggested two singles, but

Amanda didn't want to be alone. On the one hand she was jittery and on the other she tore my clothes off me as soon as we were in the room.

This time it was short, hard and, frankly, a little bleak. I didn't enjoy finding dead people, it was detrimental to my libido. Amanda needed sex to relieve the tension. Either that or she was just plain perverse.

Eventually we fell asleep and slept too long. We just had time for a quick breakfast at one of the estimated 98 bakeries in the Altstadt, then off we went. The Citadel always opens at 10 o'clock in the morning on 365 days a year. The only entrance was, as befits a proper castle, on the moat bridge.

The Citadel was astonishingly beautiful for a fort that was built only for defense and drill purposes. Red brick was dominant, it was not a simple fortress but surprisingly elegant, revealing its High Renaissance Italian roots. The square foundations with the large parade ground culminate in "bastions" at all four corners, arrow-shaped annexes from which aggressors, not visible from the castle wall, could be slaughtered (it didn't work with Napoleon, the commander capitulated immediately). The bastions are called: "King", "Queen", "Prince" and "Brandenburg". We wanted to visit the King.

The King's Bastion is annexed to the Julius Tower, the only Citadel tower. I learned later, the tower was built centuries before the Citadel and is probably the oldest building in Berlin that is not a church. I found particularly appropriate that until 1918 the Julius Tower had housed the "Reichskriegsschatz", war reparations paid by the bloody French. I reckon that's enough history for now. What I found most interesting was that parts of the best Edgar Wallace film were shot here: *The Ringer*.

Our war chest was not in the tower but in the center of the bastion.

"Will you get a move on?" Amanda complained, she had swung into action immediately. We had taken a detour and although, apart from us, only a small handful of tourists was there, we were not alone.

"Will you behave more conspicuously?" I muttered back. We finally arrived at our destination, the "King Bastion", which was in the south-west of the Citadel, almost next to the entrance gate. The sun peeked out from behind the clouds, everything was quiet and peaceful and there was no one here but us. In today's peaceful world, the Bastion is just a beautiful green area, surrounded by masonry. I liked it. Guess who couldn't care less.

"Here it is," said Amanda, and pointed excitedly to a mound that was covered with trees. At the foot of some stone stairs there were two gravestones, which suggested it was a burial mound - unfortunately without the monoliths. Amanda rushed up, I trotted slowly behind. I was quite nervous, but on the other hand I'm a pretty cool guy. You have to demonstrate it now and then otherwise no one will believe it.

Jan had described to us in detail where the case was and even marked it on the flyer Citadel visitors were given. The cross marked this hill. At the top we found two wooden benches and a strange structure that looked like a frame for swings. Of course, the hooks under the crossbar were too weak to take children, so I guessed it was a kind of barbecue: dead chickens or similar creatures were hung here and sizzled over an open fire. Slllrrrpp.

"Will you stop staring at that shit, loser?"

Amanda was impatient. She had already turned her attention to one of the trees growing on the hill. Don't ask me what kind of tree – the important thing was that the branches were intertwined. Actually, it was probably several trees that had somehow grown into each other. It looked picturesque and mysterious - and was a good hiding place for something the size of a suitcase.

"I think I see something!" Amanda declared, while I carefully checked if anyone was watching us. But the coast was clear.

Amanda climbed up and was poking around among the branches. Her gorgeous ass hung in front me and the expectant trembling buttocks reminded me of something, but I couldn't pursue it right now.

"There it is!" shrieked Amanda, as quietly as her feelings would allow. "I've found it!"

I supported her by holding her butt (always the gentleman), and she grabbed something that had been hidden in the depths of the tree. I helped her down. She giggled and chuckled as if she were drunk, she held a metal case in her hand.

"I've got it... I've got it... I've got it..."

She took it in both hands and held it high, exhausted from the effort. Then she put the object of her desire on the wooden bench next to the tree. We sat on each side. She ignored me and fiddled around with the suitcase.

It was smaller than expected, and flatter, more the size of a briefcase. It may originally have been a case for an exclusive firearm, was entirely of metal and had a complicated combination lock. I understood why Jan and Nowak would not or could not force it open. That could only be done with the code or brute strength and, not knowing what was inside, they hadn't wanted to take any unnecessary risks. I thought of my "Detlev-purse", which was in the Astra. It would take me a while to do it, but it could be done.

"We can't open it here," I told Amanda, "let's go."

She nodded and even allowed me to carry the loot. Not because she trusted me, but because the suitcase was really heavy. Suddenly she was gentle and affectionate again. We kissed as we left the bastion and I suggested we climb the Julius Tower now that we were here. Amanda agreed. Suddenly, she had all the time in the world.

We climbed the wooden staircase that curled around the inner wall to the top of the round tower. Tourists come here primarily to visit the Julius tower. We had a great view of the Altstadt of Spandau from the observation deck, the sky was so clear we could see as far as Berlin. The Funkturm and the former CIA monitoring station on Teufelsberg were visible. My Berlin. I would never leave here.

I propped the suitcase against the battlements.

"It's incredibly heavy," I said. "It's not money in there."

Amanda smiled at me. "Sure, you've made your point. If we can't flog the stuff, we'll rake in the reward." I put my arm around her.

"You are so relaxed right now," I found, "it really suits you."

"Thanks Babe," she said, and we kissed. The world lay at our feet, we had achieved a common goal.

We caught our breath and looked at each other.

"I don't want it to end here," I said cautiously. I'm not good at such things. Think Arnold Schwarzenegger ice-skating.

"It doesn't have to," she said.

"We may have to go underground. Kropf isn't likely to write off his trunk in a hurry and they know that I'm involved. One more reason to go to the authorities."

"With money in our pockets, we can settle anywhere, darling."

Darling, had we already reached that stage? Well, we had found a treasure and were in a castle tower. That could almost be defined as "romantic". And it wasn't even cheesy.

I wouldn't say it anyway. It had to come from her. And it did.

"I think I love you, Phil," Amanda breathed softly and looked at the floor. She wasn't good at this stuff either.

I pulled her towards me and kissed her. She dug her tongue in my throat, with one hand in my hair and the other between my legs. I had my hands all over her; we forgot everything around us, even the trunk. Well, I did.

"Let's go," I finally gasped.

"I love it when you give orders," Amanda cooed.

We made our way to the Astra and my burglar equipment which would cope well the lock. What then happened depended on the suitcase contents.

I had parked the Astra in a parking lot, a few minutes from the Citadel. It belonged to the Art School there and was a bit secluded. We strolled leisurely to the car, there wasn't a soul around. I noticed them as I unlocked the driver's door, but it was too late.

"Good morning, Herr Eckstein," a male voice said

from behind me.

"Good morning, Fräulein Luft," another.

The phrase "the blood froze in my veins" is nonsense. That's not how it feels. "Shitting yourself" is more like it.

I wanted to turn around and grab my gun, but my shooting hand was carrying a heavy suitcase and burly Schorsch was right behind me. He must have been lurking behind the VW bus parked next to me.

I felt the gun barrel in my back.

"No funny business, dude," grunted Schorsch, "we're alone, no one can hear you yell."

I looked around for Amanda. She was on the other side of the car, Matze had twisted her arm against her back and held a knife to her throat.

Checkmate.

"I recognized your lousy jalopy," Schorsch said brightly, "you parked it in front of the *Flamingo* the other day. Good to see you both. And especially that beautiful piece of luggage."

"How did you fi..." The question stuck my throat because the answer was clear.

"That cock sucking Polack," said Schorsch a tad politically incorrect, "got completely plastered and forgot to split. That's how unhealthy booze is."

"But at least he didn't feel anything," interjected Matze, "so cutting his throat wasn't too unpleasant."

I could see some rust brown spots on his suit jacket. It had obviously been quite a messy affair. Poor Jan, maybe I should have looked after him. But he was a grown man, a criminal. I wasn't his dad.

"Thanks for doing the work for us," said Schorsch and grabbed the suitcase from my hand. "Unfortunately, the ass pirate didn't tell us the exact location. *Someone* lost his self-control."

"It wasn't my fault!" Matze protested. "He grinned so stupidly as if he was hot for me."

"You messed things up," replied his companion. "We may have to sink the whole damn ship!"

Amanda stood there stunned. She looked at the suitcase she had owned for a fleeting moment. I had never seen her so sad, so utterly desperate.

"Okay," I said to Schorsch, "take it and fuck off."

He said nothing, just fished the gun out of my jacket.

"Cute," he laughed, "it probably really hurts, at least when you get it over your head."

I felt a very familiar thump on the back of my head, it was still very sore, and then the lights went out.

A suitcase full of blood

By now I was really annoyed.

Am I Berlin's punching bag? Not even gay demonstrators in Russia are beaten up as often as I am. I don't want to be a wimp, but my skull is made of flesh and bone and my brain consists of... well, brain.

Everything really ached. It was a lot worse than when I woke up next to Peter Brecht on the factory floor. I was out for more than twenty minutes. I couldn't prove it though. I found myself in a wood-paneled small room. There was a whole lot of stuff lying around, including dumbbells, lights, a fan and a few boxes, a storage room with no windows. I was bound hand and foot to a chair and my overcoat was missing. At least I wasn't gagged and, apart from a king-sized headache, seemed to have no further injuries. Perhaps they felt I had suffered enough. It was more likely, however, that the real pain hadn't started yet.

I heard voices on the other side of the door. Voices that I now knew well.

"What about the girl?" That was Matze.

"Maybe later," said Schorsch, "when the boss has had his fun."

"Mind-blowing boobs."

"Awesome ass."

"Shall we do her together?"

"Sure, why not..."

Because its suppressed homosexuality, I thought, even though thinking was difficult. Amanda was still alive, that was clear and so was I, which was a bit surprising.

"What about the Jew?" Matze now asked.

Yes, what about the Jew?

"The boss will want to use the lawn mower again."

Silence.

My heart missed a beat and the two gangsters didn't seem enthusiastic either.

"Do I have to watch?" asked Matze. "I mean, it's really..."

"Make an excuse," said Schorsch. "I'll check on him."

The door opened, and Schorsch came. Matze disappeared.

"Ah, you're awake," he said as he came in. He crouched in front of me and looked me in the eye and the terrible thing was, he really pitied me. I was totally fucked up.

"Listen, mate," he said slowly, "I have to say it again – you have only yourself to blame. For this and what is coming. We gave you a stark warning when we beat you up. You don't mess with Hartmut Kropf. It's your own fault, you know?"

Yes, I knew. I was personally responsible for the consequences of my actions after being thrashed and then lied to good and proper by Amanda. I couldn't even blame my penis. It was a deadly mix of greed and the urge to be a hero.

"Got a cigarette?" I asked, ignoring his lecture.

"Sure, I still have got a few of yours."

He pulled out the *Eckstein No. 5s* which he had taken from me two days ago. He put one between my lips and gave me a light, then lit one himself and we puffed away like old friends. One of whom was tied to a chair.

"What time is it?" I asked.

"Eleven-ish. You slept pretty long. Surprised me, I didn't hit you that hard."

"Well, the previous job played a role," I growled.

"What do you mean? I didn't hit you on the head."

"I mean in the factory."

Schorsch frowned. "What're you talking about?"

I was about to answer when Matze came in.

"We have to take him in."

They untied me and pulled me to my feet. The architecture looked familiar and shortly after I was in the huge loft which Hartmut Kropf had built for himself. They put me in the same leather chair as before and stood guard over me. I could see through the skylight that it was already dark and raining heavily.

"Hey, Jew," Hartmut Kropf greeted me from his desk. The case was on the table with other stuff. It was still closed and seemed to be causing Kropf a headache even bigger than mine and I was pretty sure I had concussion. I could barely think straight.

"You don't happen to know the combination, do you? This lock is a real bugger. I could drill it open, but shit, that might cause damage in the six-or seven-figure range."

"I would love to help you," I said heavily, "it breaks my heart to say it, but I don't have the combination."

"I know, Jew, I know. Not you. But the beautiful Amanda, right?"

"She didn't mention it to me."

Kropf laughed.

"Yes, she doesn't tell anyone much, right? And if she does, they're usually fairy tales. What story did she dish up so you'd look for Peter?"

"That her brother was missing."

"For God's sake. The things those two got up to are

taboo between brothers and sisters. Call me a prude if you like."

"You're a prude."

He grinned. Then he looked over to the lawn mower I noticed on my first visit, sitting quietly in a corner.

"Oh man, this'll be fun."

I tried to concentrate. "Where's Amanda?"

"She's recovering," he winked at me. "To be honest, I can understand why you were fooled by her. She does good stuff to you and tags along everywhere. But I wouldn't have given her any choice, the little whore."

I tried to block out the intrusive images. I felt sick and I was frightened. If I wanted to leave here alive, I must not to show it.

"What the heck is in the suitcase," I asked.

"You don't know? Amanda knows. She didn't say a word?"

"No."

"Shall I get her? Maybe you have a few farewell words for her?"

It was probably not a serious suggestion, but I said yes anyway. Matze left the room and came back two minutes later with Amanda in tow. She was wearing only a bathrobe.

"Hello, Phil..."

She croaked more than spoke. Her face was badly bruised; would shimmer in all colors of the rainbow tomorrow - if she was still alive tomorrow. Her left eye was swollen shut and Matze had to support her otherwise she would have fallen over.

Matze and Schorsch put Amanda on the couch when they realized that she couldn't stand upright. I could see that their appetite for the projected threesome had vanished. The "right of the first night" for the Lord of the Manor was a tradition that had died out with good reason.

Kropf said nothing in the meantime; he was busy with the suitcase. He had all kinds of utensils on the table but hadn't accomplished anything. He sighed, got up and came over to us. He crouched down next to Amanda and turned her head towards his.

"Here's a conciliatory proposal, babe," he said quietly. "It's fair to say, I always keep my word. You and me, we've had our fun. I can bump you off right away or shave you a little bit" - he pointed to the lawn mower - "or just let you go. Give me the combination. If you know it, out with it. Peter knew it. He had to check the contents on site. He must have told you, after all you were a team."

She opened her eyes, her gaze was directed at me. She asked me for forgiveness with that look.

"Four. Seven. Six. Two. One. Three. Nine. Five."

She said the numbers slowly, like a memorized poem.

Kropf jumped up and ran to the suitcase. He put it in front of him on the coffee table and sat in the armchair.

"Again," he growled.

She dictated the combination again and he set the lock accordingly. You could hear the clicks. The case sprang open and Kropf took a deep breath. Schorsch and Matze were also curious but didn't let either Amanda or me out of sight.

Kropf slowly lifted the cover.

"Oh man..." whispered Kropf, awe written all over his face. The lighting in the loft was good, it fell on the suitcase contents and threw a reflection on his face. The contents of the suitcase seemed to glow.

"Holy shit," marveled Schorsch, who peeked around the corner. If he hadn't had his gun in his hand - a pretty heavy thing - it would have been a good moment for me to turn things round. But it wasn't the right moment. I wanted to know what all the fuss had been about.

Kropf solemnly turned the suitcase so we could all see what was in it. Matze craned his neck and half-dead Amanda looked up and blinked sluggishly towards the coffee table.

I found it difficult to recognize immediately what it was. It glittered so much it seemed almost like a hallucination. I have also mentioned my concussion.

"Do you know what this is, Jew?" Kropf asked.

"Yes," I said, "diamonds. Hundreds of them."

"Exactly one thousand," the gangster boss informed me, and his hands trembled. "Every single one worth least 20,000 Euros."

Amanda whimpered. But not in pain.

I would never ever have kept the gemstones. There would be a handsome reward if they were returned to their rightful owners. But that was now academic.

"This suitcase is worth twenty million," Kropf enthused. "My fee is twenty percent. I'll take my share of bling and the rest goes to our client in America. It's a great feeling when you've done a good job."

"Congratulations," I mumbled. I had to think about something quickly in order to buy time. "Where are the stones from?"

"West Africa, you twat," said Kropf and rummaged around greedily with both hands in the sparkling stones. "There are militias and rebels who need a lot of money for weapons. My esteemed client delivers them and is paid in gemstones. Not exactly a bargain, but niggers can't get their heads around that."

"Blood diamonds," I said. That is the term used for diamonds that are sold to fund armed conflict, of all the deals in the world probably the dirtiest.

He looked up.

"Yes, well-named. Blood diamonds. Lots of little black children were and are slaughtered for this, I guess. This is a suitcase full of blood. It sparkles magnificently. I feel like a vampire!"

He delved around in his riches. I still had no plan. And I gave up. If I had to die, I'd like to do it in an upright way.

"Can I go now, please? I think I left the iron on."

Kropf laughed.

"You know, Jew, I'm in a good mood and you're a funny guy. I'm actually tempted to let you go, you and the girl. But as the saying goes - you know too much."

"You gave Amanda your word."

"All right, all right. But we are allowed to lie as much as we like to a hypocritical bitch like her. That's my personal code of honor."

I had to admit there was something to be said for that.

"Matze, get Berta!" Kropf ordered the gangster. It didn't take long to guess who Berta was because Matze made a beeline for the old-fashioned, petrol-driven lawn mower and drove it into the middle of the large room. He didn't look too happy doing it.

Meanwhile Schorsch had changed his position so that he had a clean line of fire. He took no notice of Amanda, she was obviously not a danger to anyone. She just stared paralyzed at the suitcase and I saw a tear running down her disfigured face.

"Lying on his back or belly?" Schorsch asked his boss.

"On his back," and looked at me with cold, dead eyes. "I'll start by shaving off his balls and cock. And the little bitch can eat them."

Schorsch pulled a face I couldn't interpret. But it was clear he didn't share his boss' passions, neither did Matze. But he daren't help me. No-one can afford to show weakness in front of his boss.

"Get up," Schorsch said softly to me, "and lie down in front of the handcuffs."

I now saw that in the middle of the wooden floor were handcuffs attached to chains. They hadn't been there on my first visit. They probably came out for special occasions only.

"Boss," Matze volunteered, his voice breaking, "I just remembered, shouldn't I take care of the boat with the two Polacks?"

"Later," muttered the crop and continued playing with the gems. "Maybe not at all. You were wearing gloves, right?"

"Yes, but you know, DNA evidence and stuff..."

Kropf turned to Matze.

"Your problem. You messed up. You got fobbed off with the wrong suitcase and nearly let the other ass bandit escape."

"Boss, seriously, we need to take care of the boat," Schorsch joined in, he seemed to have a higher standing with Kropf. I was still sitting in my chair. My senses were working as best they could, given the circumstances and my injuries.

Kropf sighed.

“Well okay, we'll finish off our friend here now and then you can clear off and clean up.”

“I can steer a boat,” said Matze, “I learned it in the military. We'll sink it somewhere in Brandenburg.”

“Great,” Kropf nodded. “Why isn't the Jew on the floor yet?”

Schorsch came nearer and pulled me up, with his gun pointed at my heart.

"Your own fault," he growled again softly, "you bloody idiot."

He resented having to watch me being torn to pieces. That was my only chance of escape.

"Shoot me," I begged him in a whisper. Then it would be over quickly. Schorsch squinted.

"What are you two beauties whispering about?" Kropf shouted indignantly; he had mounted Berta in the meantime and placed his hand on the starter cord.

"He wants me to kill him quickly and painlessly," said Schorsch, without letting me out of sight. "Sorry, pal, but I'll only shoot you here," he said to me and pointed the gun at my crotch. "That won't make the next half hour any more bearable." He turned to Kropf. "Should he undress?"

Kropf thought for a second.

"Nope," he said, "Berta cuts through clothes. Remember that Turk, how I worked from the head to toe..."

"Yes, boss," interrupted Schorsch, who remembered only too well. "That was cool."

VRRRRRROOOOOOMMMMMMMMMMMM!!!

Kropf had set the machine in motion and it made a dreadful din. I heard the music being turned up in the bar downstairs. They knew what was coming.

Chugchugchugchugchugchug...

Poor innocent Berta, the killing machine, chugged peacefully waiting for me to resign myself to my fate.

Maybe I did deserve this. I should have informed Lisa Becker, I should have handed Amanda over to her. Then the authorities could have secured the gems and maybe even have jailed Hartmut Kropf, the unhinged murderer and torturer. Now he was free to continue his reign of terror and torture people to death. People like me.

"Get down," Schorsch ordered and threw me on my back. Matze had moved as far away as possible and didn't help his colleague; he awaited the upcoming event in the background. Kropf waited patiently while Schorsch put the first handcuff around my right wrist.

Even today I wonder whether Amanda had waited for this moment or whether she had just regained consciousness.

The next thing I heard was Matze yell.

"Boss, the bitch!"

Kropf and Schorsch swung around. Amanda was no longer on the sofa.

And the suitcase had vanished.

Matze ran – in the direction of an open door on the other side of the loft. The heavy iron door through which we had come was, of course, guarded by something muscular on the other side, so that was the only escape route - if it was an escape route at all and not just an adjoining room. I caught a glimpse of Amanda's bathrobe as she disappeared.

"Get her!" Kropf shouted beside herself with rage. He probably meant Matze but Schorsch also responded and was, for a moment, too confused to pay attention to me.

A second later, I had his gun in my hand. I could even see the brand: Beretta, fully automatic, the type which shot three times in a row, almost a machine gun, a really nasty, dirty gun that shouldn’t exist at all. However, with it in my hand, at this particular moment, I didn't care to be too judgmental.

Schorsch looked at me in panic.

“Look mate, I... please...”

I shot him in the kneecap. A single shot, but it was sufficient.

“Aaaaaiiiiiiiiiiiiiiihhhhh!!!”

His bloodcurdling shriek reminded Kropf of my existence. I tried to get up while a frenzied Schorsch rolled on the floor and screamed and shook helplessly in unbearable pain.

“Fucking Jew! I'll kill you,” shouted Kropf. He gripped the handle of the lawn mower and would certainly have run over me a second later, but I rolled to the side. My right hand was still handcuffed but Kropf missed me and I turned around.

Kropf realized his situation was hopeless, he had lost. He did the only thing he could: Ran away.

“Don't move,” I shouted and fired. If I had been in better shape, Kropf would've had three bullets in the cerebrum. But I was in bad shape and didn't know how to handle that vicious weapon. The bullets smashed into the frame of the back door through which Kropf escaped, like Amanda before him with Matze at her heels.

I was alone in the room with Schorsch, who was in no fit state to do anything. He moaned and howled in agony, blood streaming from his leg, I felt sorry for him.

“Give me the key to the handcuffs,” I yelled at him. "Now, or I'll kill you!"

“In... my... Jaaaaaackeeet,” Schorsch howled. Oh yes, nothing hurts more than a shattered kneecap. Or having a baby. Or passing a kidney stone.

He lay close enough for me get at his jacket, I fished around a bit for the key in the side pocket. A few seconds later, I was free and up on my own two feet.

What now?

I checked the gun. It was charged, except for the three used cartridges, and in single-shot mode. I left it at that though I would have felt better with my little Walther P22.

"Where's my stuff?" I asked Schorsch and he pointed to the back door.

"Behind... the door... cupboard..." he gasped. "Please... Ambulance... Please, mate..."

"I'll think about it," I replied, and hurried through the door through which a blonde, a diamond case and two gangsters had disappeared - and I wanted to join them.

Past the door was a small room with a simple, wooden spiral staircase that led up to the roof apparently. My coat, with my P22 in it, hung in a closet. I put it on, secured and stowed away the Beretta and pulled out my small caliber pistol. It felt damn good. All the endorphin released into my blood in the face of death meant I was nothing short of euphoric. I was ready for the showdown.

I heard voices upstairs. I got to a small door leading to the roof. It was dark outside, but the neon sign with the big blue flamingo, which I had never noticed before, shed an eerie light. It was raining heavily so visibility was limited.

I could now hear the voices more clearly. I moved forward and then I saw them.

Amanda had taken refuge near some large chimneys.

Maybe she thought she could hide there or even climb down them - in times of stress you have the funniest thoughts. She should have looked for the fire escape.

Kropf had just found her and stumbled towards her. Matze was with him. I couldn't remember whether he had a gun or not.

"Give me the suitcase, you stupid bitch," roared Kropf. Amanda looked at me with a big smile. *Thanks baby.*

"You were supposed to guard the door," Kropf screamed at Matze when he saw me.

He immediately reached into his jacket and pulled out a gun.

"Bump him off!" snapped Kropf.

It was dark, rainy, and I had concussion. I repeat it just to give you an idea of how outstanding my performance was.

The shot from my "girl's gun" hit Matze right in the heart. He reared up and dropped his gun. It slid towards me and I kicked it away. A second shot landed simultaneously in Matze's skull.

It had finally happened. I had shot a man dead.

It wasn't a good feeling, even though it was in self-defense. I was in shock for a few seconds and couldn't keep an eye on the rest of the workforce. Kropf took advantage of that and when I came to my senses he had Amanda in a stranglehold, he could've broken her neck with a single jerk. He snatched the case with the other hand.

The two stood there. Amanda's naked body was only half covered by the bathrobe. She was trembling and moaning, could hardly breathe and not at all move. Kropf grinned at me, the grin was not triumphant, more the snarl of an injured Khan who wanted to spit his last breath on Captain Kirk.

"Hey, Eckstein," he exclaimed. Suddenly I was no longer "Jew". He waved the suitcase from side to side. We were about ten meters apart. "How about a deal?"

"I'm all ears," I called back, even though I had already decided that Kropf wouldn't leave this roof alive. It's absolutely true when they say the first kill is the hardest, after that it gets easier and easier.

"I could just throw the bitch off the roof," he began, and I realized he was right, the drop behind them fell straight into the yard. "Or I could break her neck, no problem for me!"

I now listened to him more carefully.

"Or we forget the whole business and part as friends. You get as many diamonds as you want, you also get the bitch! Then you simply do a runner! Then we both make good!"

I didn't answer. Amanda's eyes were imploring.

"Come on!" Kropf shouted, angry because I hesitated. "The biggest deal you'll ever have! Stop messing about, Jew! Money's the only thing that counts for you!"

Eloquently argued, Herr Kropf. I lowered the gun.

"Okay," I said, grinning broadly, "you're right. You know us Jews all too well."

Kropf laughed and pulled Amanda in my direction. He dragged her over Matze's dead body, gave it a kick and stopped ten meters in front of me.

"Come on, put the gun away," he said, in an attempt to regain authority.

I threw down the P22 and heard it hit the ground.

"Don't fuck around," I warned him. "Let the whore

go."

Kropf cooperated and Amanda collapsed. I saw that she had lost consciousness.

"The suitcase," I said next. Next to us was a chimney with metal cover, Kropf placed the object of our desires on it. We assessed each other. We were probably equally strong. Hand to hand combat would end... who knew how? I could see he was thinking the same thing.

I knew of course that he wouldn't dream of giving me a single diamond.

"So..." he muttered, and his hand slid towards the suitcase. He grabbed it and swung it in my direction.

I had seen this coming and jumped backwards. It was time to end this farce. I pulled out my trump card – Schorsch's vicious Beretta.

Kropf paused. He froze before my eyes. His blue eyes gleamed almost ultramarine in the light of the Flamingo. His mouth twitched. He looked at me.

"You won't shoot me," he claimed with plenty of misplaced optimism. "You're the good, shining hero. You want to save the girl. I don't begrudge you that. You want the gems. Well okay, then I miss out on the big haul, but I have got other irons in the fire."

He turned towards the door.

"I shall leave now," he said softly, and turned his back to me as he slowly moved away. "Don't shoot me in the back. That would never count as self-defense, how would you explain that to the cops?"

The man knew all the tricks, that at least deserved respect. He went on his way unperturbed. I said nothing.

"I'm getting out of here, Jew. You win, you shining hero. You're the good guy and I'm the villain. You beat me. Just like a fairy tale."

He wittered on.

"I surrender before the better man," he continued. "Anyone else would finish me off. Especially after what I've done to your babe, to all her holes..."

He paused.

It was his last mistake.

I didn't shoot him. He was right, it would have been difficult to sell that as self-defense.

Instead, I tossed the gun aside, which I hadn't yet released, grabbed Kropf by the neck and twisted his right arm backwards. He couldn't defend himself as I dragged him to the roof edge.

It wasn't difficult to throw him down. It was all over, and when he fell off the building onto the street, we both knew he wouldn't survive. He didn't cry out. He didn't flail with his arms. He accepted his fate.

The impact was almost inaudible.

Epilogue

"Give me a reason not to put you in the clink," Lisa Becker demanded. We were sitting in an interview room in the State Criminal Investigation Department. Her colleague, Fabian Zonk, had joined us, a sporty, silent guy who, as I knew, regularly desecrated Lisa's extensive body.

"What are you on about?" I asked rebelliously. "I delivered a bunch of criminals to your doorstep."

"Two of them dead."

"That'll save the paperwork. And the court hearings. Don't bother to thank me."

Zonk interrupted.

"Eckstein, you hid a criminal from us."

"The way you say that sounds really negative. Why don't we say, I protected a frightened, persecuted innocent?"

"You withheld valuable information from us," he continued, "in order to profit from a felony."

Hmm. The guy was absolutely straight, a true policeman. And Lisa wasn't any different.

"Blood diamonds, you bastard!" Lisa glowered. "That's absolutely disgusting! I'm really disappointed in you."

"Let me say in my defense: I had no idea. Besides, I would have handed over the stones to you. Honestly, I give you my word!"

Lisa und Zonk looked at each other.

"Now that you mention it," muttered Zonk, "we spoke to Georg Kramer."

I was confused. "To whom?"

"You know him as Schorsch."

“Oh yes, how is he?”

“He will never be able to walk properly,” said Lisa. “The Beretta is a really mean gun.”

“It was his own gun. That's biblical justice.”

“Oh yes, justice, I just wanted to mention that,” Zonk continued. “He confirmed most of your story. He also said that, according to his deceased employer, the case contained precisely one thousand diamonds.”

“Is that what he said?”

“Well, we counted them,” Lisa smiled sweetly, “and you know what, Phillie-Billie? We found only nine hundred and ninety.”

I said nothing.

“Would you like to comment, Phillie-Billie?” asked Zonk.

“I’m not sure what to say. Maybe it wasn't exactly a thousand right from the beginning. Maybe some were diverted en route. Perhaps an official took advantage of a favorable moment. That's all I can think of.”

The two looked at each other again. They were not at all pleased. I thought they should be grateful, after all a number of murders had been solved and a suitcase with diamonds worth twenty million had been secured - and they were treating me like a criminal.

“Furthermore, Kramer adamantly denies having anything to do with the death of Peter Brecht.”

“Oh really?”

“Oh yes!” Zonk thundered, he was getting impatient. “I warn you, Eckstein, we could...”

“What?” I interrupted him. “What could you do?”

Lisa took a deep breath – which worked wonders not only on me but also on her quick-tempered colleague.

God, how could her bra stand it?

"Fabian," she said softly to Zonk, "would you leave us alone for a minute?"

Yes, give us fifteen minutes, I thought to myself, but somehow I didn't believe that was what Lisa had in mind. When Zonk was outside, Lisa leaned forward on her elbows and looked at me searchingly.

"What do you think? Who killed Peter Brecht?"

I was afraid of this question, but I had an honest answer to it.

"I don't know, Lisa. Schorsch seemed to know nothing about Brecht, I mentioned it to him and he had no idea what I was talking about. He's probably telling the truth."

"Was it your sugar baby?"

"How is she?"

"Terrible. Kropf was really a fucking sadist. Off the record: Thank you for pushing him off the roof."

"It was pure self-defense, Frau Kommissar."

"Of course," Lisa smiled, "of course. No one would doubt that."

"Will I be charged?"

"The prosecutor is talking about obstruction of an investigation."

"What a nerve."

"He's absolutely right. I accept that you didn't notice that the blonde took you for a ride. Whether we would have found the suitcase is open to discussion. The *Zuzanna* was more of a fluke, if we're honest. But you should definitely have called us when you found Pawel Nowak's dead body."

"I left that to Jan," I defended myself, "honestly, I told him to call the police."

"In the tacit hope that he wouldn't."

I grinned. Lisa was too smart for me. I really liked her. If only that damn Zonk weren't around...

"You were aware of the location of stolen property worth tens of millions," added Lisa. "The only thing that might get you off is your heroic performance in the *Blue Flamingo*. We would never have caught Kropf. He always covered his tracks. Even if we had caught his minions collecting the suitcase - he would have wriggled himself out of it. He was damn clever for a psychopath. To be honest, you're in the good books of the entire Berlin police force."

I smiled to myself. That would prove useful in future.

"What about Amanda?"

Lisa shrugged her shoulders.

"She was involved in a criminal conspiracy, she'll probably get two years. We'll do our best to find her DNA in the KFW-factory, but I'm not too optimistic. Do you suppose she would be prepared to kill her lover because she didn't want to go halves?"

I didn't need to think.

"Absolutely."

We were silent.

"Maybe there were other reasons," Lisa speculated. "Maybe he wanted to get rid of her or leave. What I don't understand is: Why did she lead you to the body? It's the only interpretation, with all the photo clues placed decoratively in Brecht's apartment."

"She may have taken fright at her own courage. She needed a protector, didn't want to be alone against those gangsters. If she killed Brecht... what did she use?"

"A large-caliber Glock," Lisa replied, "we didn't find

the gun."

"It probably belonged to Brecht. If Amanda did it, it was perhaps on impulse. She needed me as a detective to find the suitcase. Then she conned me and knocked me up so I didn't suspect her and in order to motivate me more or wake my protective instincts, something like that. Perhaps Brecht hadn't given her all the details. Why she chose the factory, I can't say, maybe it was intended as a meeting place between him and Nowak or Kropf. Maybe Brecht had lured Amanda there to eliminate her because he reckoned he didn't really need her and she tricked him somehow."

"Then we'll definitely find her DNA."

There was a knock and Zonk came in. He did not look at me.

"Can you spare me a minute?"

Lisa left me alone with my thoughts. And my aches. I was so completely up the spout I prescribed myself a four-week break, either in a cell or in the Caribbean.

It had been an eventful few days. Five of people I had met were now dead. I could see the dawn through the window. It was Friday. Amanda came into my life on Monday evening. I didn't regret that at all. Not many women trigger more than a twitch in my loins. I refused to think about *love*. The word had been slaughtered by the entertainment industry and had no longer any real meaning. We have to find a new term that describes the stomach turning feeling, where you would do anything for another person, even without a reward. The irrepressible urge to be with someone. The surrender of reason. I promised myself one thing:

That will never, ever happen to me again!

Lisa came back and sat down. Zonk stood in the doorway.

“Amanda Luft made a full confession in relation to the murder of Peter Brecht. She said you had no idea and that she deceived you, because she needed your help as a protector and detective.”

“And stallion,” Zonk added gruffly.

“Jealous?” I asked, but that was nonsense. Zonk was allowed to grope Lisa's massive breasts, he didn't envy any man in the world.

“This confession will mitigate her sentence,” said Lisa, “she knew that. My colleague only needed to whip out his notebook when she woke up.”

“She's a smart girl,” I commented. “How much do you think she'll get?”

“Five to eight years. Will you wait that long for her?”

“No.”

“Clever boy.”

“No. I'm an Idiot.”

“Put that in the protocol,” Zonk said and left. Lisa and I stood up and for some reason she gave me a hug. Felt really good, all these butter-soft curves on my broken body.

“If ever you leave Captain Sexy Ass,” I said softly, “you know where I live.”

“You are on my long list,” Lisa smiled. “I'm going to visit Amanda at the Urban Clinic. Want to come?”

I considered briefly.

“No.”

I trudged from the Landeskriminalamt to Wittenbergplatz in a light drizzle. My bones ached, and I missed feeling my P22 in my side. Hopefully I would get it back soon, though I wasn't really sure if I wanted it back.

I had killed a man with it - Matze. It was self-defense, that always presupposed that one's own life was the most important. A natural instinct. It also meant that I killed a second man though it hadn't been absolutely necessary.

Something had happened to me that night and I didn't like it. I was now a different person. Certainly not a better one.

The *KaDeWe* loomed up in front of me, grey and depressing as all Cathedrals of Commerce are. I thought of the ten stones hidden in the alley next to the *Blue Flamingo*, where I first met Schorsch and Matze's fists. Some ne'er-do-well had hidden the bling there. Two hundred thousand Euros. I would be able to flog them easily, what else are contacts for?

But they were blood diamonds. The money the "owners" got was used to buy weapons that wreaked carnage. I would definitely not be the good guy in the story if I kept the money - I would be no better than Kropf, or Amanda.

I urgently had to do something for my soul.

I didn't know yet what would happen to the remaining gemstones; as far as I was concerned *Amnesty International* and *Doctors Without Borders* could soon count on substantial anonymous donations. Maybe a fancy smartphone was in it for me, or a Kindle Fire, it looked truly stylish. And some compensation for injuries suffered.

I make no claim to a halo. Have I mentioned that?

Postscript

Philip Eckstein is a tribute to the greatest detective ever devised by a writer: Lazlo Woodbine. You've probably never read any of his antics but don't worry, nobody else has either. He is the brainchild of a brilliant writer, Robert Rankin. However, Lazlo crops up in the sidelines because, in Rankin's universe, he is only a fictional character, created by the fictional crime novelist P.P. Penrose. This is known as "metafiction".

Philip also owes his name to him because Woodbine, like Eckstein, is a cigarette brand. As a non-smoker I find it difficult to advertise for tobacco, but detectives in the *Noir* tradition always smoke. He had to be named Philip, not only because of the most famous representative of the trade, Philip Marlowe, but also for Philip Kerr, my favorite thriller writer.

Certain rules apply with Lazlo Woodbine, and I've tried to conform with as many as possible. I barely describe Philip's appearance - so every (at least male) reader can imagine himself as Philip Eckstein. The narrative rules for Woodbine, however, are so strict that I couldn't meet them all, but Lazlo himself probably violated them repeatedly in "reality".

In the final analysis, Lazlo Woodbine is not a genuine detective and that's how I see Philip Eckstein. No detective in 21st Century Berlin would behave that way. This is about fun and gripping entertainment and I hope it has given you some pleasure.

Cameron Strike

If you enjoyed this book, please check out these other novels by Cameron Strike

Devil's Mountain

Berlin Noir #2

by Cameron Strike

A young American turns up at Philip Eckstein's office, claiming that he gets persecuted by the NSA. Philip tries to get rid of him in an elegant way - until it turns out that he is telling the truth. An incited Philip runs from one shooting to the next, interrupted only by neck breaking chases and cynical verbal duels.

The big showdown takes place on the Devil's Mountain, at one of the most bizarre places that have ever existed in the world - and not just because it looks like a penis.

Decapitator

Becker & Zonk #1

by Cameron Strike

If someone lies dead in his bed, yet his head is one meter next to him, you can assume an unnatural death.

Detectives Lisa Becker and Fabian Zonk find themselves in a series of extremely bloody decapitations which seem to have no motive. However, after some time, it turns out that behind those crimes lurks a secret that changed Lisa's life forever.

Sample from

Decapitator

Juhnke was all ears as he stuffed his face with a Snickers bar – smacking his chops like a wild boar – and listened to Fabian and Lisa's report.

"The body was completely bloodless," Fabian said conversationally, "the man was chalk white. It could be that Krumm hasn't seen the sun for decades. But considering that half the bedroom was steeped in red, I reckon the body and the head are now five kilos lighter. The blood diet works for everyone."

Is he alluding to me? Lisa asked herself involuntarily.

"Was the blood dry?" asked Juhnke, as he crumpled

the Snickers wrapping and threw it towards the wastepaper basket. He missed it by a couple of meters. Rumour had it that his use of firearms was almost as accurate. No wonder that he was doing a desk job; the validity of the Dilbert Principle could be proved even at a police station.

"Yes, it was," said Lisa, "it couldn't be described as red any more. More of a Sienna-hazelnut tone."

"Thank you, Frau Becker. Your powers of observation never cease to impress me."

You've got a booger on your nose, Lisa thought. What she said was: "I would say that death occurred around 3 o'clock last night, but we'll have to wait for the autopsy. The murder weapon wasn't found, but I'm going for a kind of axe or even a particularly large butcher knife. A saw wasn't used, as the cut was very clean. The eyes were still closed, which indicates he was unaware of what happened. Moreover, no one heard screaming and there was no indication of a struggle. My personal guess: Either an act of revenge or the work of a psychopath."

"What beautiful terminology we have to hand," grinned Juhnke.

"Yes, that's what police training is all about these days," Lisa replied casually.

"You learn a lot of nonsense in training which is of no use later on."

Lisa didn't give a shit about her boss's comments. The pointed remarks about her education at the Academy were part of his usual repertoire. No one else in the department had been as heavily immersed in communication training and social sciences as she had. Of course, they knew about jurisprudence and forensic techniques, but then she had set herself other priorities. She realized very quickly that preparation for real working life was very limited at the Academy. Even now, she had the feeling that basically anyone could become a police inspector – all you needed to know were the service regulations and even they were seldom adhered to. The other thing that amazed her was that the proportion of women trained was thirty to forty percent; however, there were only about five percent in the police force. Where did they all go?

"I agree with Lisa," Fabian chimed in. "I think this was a madman. Why would anyone kill an innocent tram driver, and in such a way?"

"A hustler maybe?" Juhnke asked.

Lisa and Fabian and grinned furtively at each other. *No thanks*, they thought.

"Happens all the time in Berlin," Juhnke continued. "A gay Aidsmonger picks up a punter, goes to his place, knocks him off and cleans him out."

"Could be, I suppose," Lisa agreed reluctantly, "but I can't imagine that Herr Krumm had anything of value in his flat. It looked more like a rat-breeding farm."

"I noticed some interesting magazines," Fabian said, "mainly trade magazines examining the female bust."

Juhnke threw a glance at Lisa's torso. She immediately remembered her first conversation with the boss. "I desperately need a woman," was the first sentence she heard from him. She nearly answered, "I'm happy to believe that."

Back then, Homicide Squad 7 consisted solely of men, it was becoming embarrassing. Not to Juhnke, but to the Senator. And thus the freshly baked Oberkommissarin,

Lisa Becker, moved from the Eifel to the LKA Berlin. Juhnke would have preferred a real Berliner, but there was no one available so he grabbed "the red eco-freak from the sticks," as he later called her when she entered a room. And that wasn't her only problem in the early days; she had gained weight faster than a newborn Panda. She now had her problems under control, but not her weight.

"Well, whatever," sighed Juhnke. "The department is currently under a lot of pressure because of all the shit in the rocker milieu. The city and the police chief have given that clear priority and I agree."

"I don't know," said Fabian. "The press will go bonkers. An exotic murder like this is great, almost like an execution. They love stuff like that."

"What journalist-vermin like or dislike doesn't interest me, Zonk. That means you two will do the job. If you need help, let me know, we'll work something out. And if not, tough. It wouldn't affect me and you are not due for a promotion. Got it?"

And they were outside.

"I must say I really appreciate his straight talk," said Fabian.

"Forget it. Or would you enjoy being in his shoes?"

They walked down the hall to the office they had shared for the last six months. Fabian was a rank above Lisa, but the difference between Hauptkommissar and Oberkommissar had little more than financial significance. However, she had only recently reached that rank, whereas Fabian had at least five years experience. But maybe it didn't matter to him that much?

"I definitely do not want his job," he said, as he threw himself into his swivel chair. "I don't want to get fat really fast and become flabby. Either physically or mentally."

"Well, when it comes to fat, I'm ideally equipped," Lisa sighed a little too theatrically in the hope of hearing an indignant whaddyatalkingabout. It didn't happen.

Fabian poured himself an apple juice and then filled Lisa's outstretched glass. "So, suggestions?"

"Has Krumm's past been checked?" Lisa wanted to know.

"I asked Hoffmann to do it. He should be back soon."

"Then we must talk to Frau Schultz. She might have seen something."

"Tomorrow probably. We'll have to write a protocol," said Fabian. "But it's still early days. What do you think of her son? Still living with his mother at 44?"

"He said she was living with him."

"Nope. The caretaker says the lease is in her name; he moved in with her several years ago."

"To care for her?"

"She's perfectly healthy. Goes for a walk every day. No, I guess this guy is either gay or chronically unemployed, or both. Or a mama's boy."

Lisa grinned. "So the perfect nominee as an insane killer with a chopper."

"Sure. It happens all the time in American books and movies and they don't write any stupid shit clichés, right?"

"Can you spare a thought for the motive, before we throw the guy into the dungeon?"

Fabian shook his head listlessly. "My goodness, you're fussy today. You probably even want us to check whether he has an alibi?"

"And if he has?"

"Then it has clearly been bloody rigged. I have decided that he is the culprit and I will ignore all counterevidence."

"This has been a nice discussion."

Read more in

Decapitator

by Cameron Strike

Gone Boys

Becker & Zonk #2

by Cameron Strike

As much as Lisa Becker loves to see naked young men – alive she likes them even more.

But they are killed, and the trail leads to an artist community, in which the eccentric attendees have to hide more than one mystery. Detectives Lisa and her colleague / lover Fabian have to face the task of finding an insane killer – among a crowd of crackpots.

House of Carnage

Becker & Zonk #3

by Cameron Strike

She is lying here, dead: In a vault without blood in her body and two holes in the neck. And she wears false vampire teeth.

What begins for detectives Lisa Becker and Fabian Zonk as a cheap horror movie turns into a bizarre ghost train full of bloodless corpses, aristocratic and non-aristocratic eccentrics and vampire enthusiasts who have more than one use for blood.

32911845R00099

Printed in Great Britain
by Amazon